The Gottingen Accident

James F. Mordechai

# The Gottingen Accident

*A New Weird novella*

# Index

# Preface

What if three famous scientists with superhero powers team up to fight a villain that wants to subvert the very fabric of the Universe?

What if? All the great alternate history novels start with their author asking this basic question. Imagining our world if something different happened in the past. Because this novel is set in our world with well-known historical characters, but things took a different turn somewhere. The Germans won the First World War and the 1917 Bolshevik revolution never took place. Time is not always a straight line and sometimes it can expand and contract. Then, Charles Darwin is coeval with Marie Curie and Albert Einstein, and they are friends. But what if these scientists were able to acquire powers that were linked to their research? What if Darwin could change the evolutionary destiny of any living being or Curie could have an X-ray vision?

But these are not the only weird things you are going to read in this novella. The weirdest of them all is probably the concept of non-Euclidean geometry. First time I heard of non-Euclidean geometry was not as you might think during the geometry classes at school or the math course at the university, but reading Howard Phillips Lovecraft's masterpiece *The Call of Cthulhu*. It was then, when I was 14, that I started to dream of a world where the laws of geometry and physics were subverted. And like in *The Call of Cthulhu* even "perverted". Can geometry or even reality be evil or be able to channel malevolence? This is what happens in Lovecraft's work: perversion of geometry and reality is a main theme in Lovecraft's stories (not only in *The Call of Cthulhu* but also in *The Dreams in the Witch House*). When the main characters are exposed to non-Euclidean geometries their reaction's spectrum goes from awe to terror to pure madness. That is, what usually follows is insanity.

Writing this short novel has brought me back to that past, my past. A teenager eager to read fantastic and horror stories. I hope I was able to convey the same horror I felt reading Lovecraft's stories and at the same time entertain my reader with a non-canonical superhero story.


The author

James F. Mordechai is a *nom de plume* of an ahead-of-his-time unjustly obscure writer. He relishes in his anonymity and if you would like to interact with him you can do so through his Twitter account @jamesMordechai or email address jamesmordechai@gmail.com

# Chapter 1
## The Anisotropic Corridor

M arie was kneeling on the ground behind a pile of broken wooden furniture; mostly desks, chairs and cabinets that once held glassware for chemistry experiments. It was, in fact, an improvised trench made of random objects found in the department. Beakers and broken flasks were scattered on the floor, some smashed into pieces, some still intact. A desk was blocking her line of sight and she couldn't see the enemy behind it.

She leaned forward for a brief moment, then she pulled her head back, disgusted. She could smell something unmistakably rotten in the box in front of her. The wooden box had a couple of badly kept ropes used as straps. She swore the bad smell was coming from that box. Did he keep a corpse in there? His wife cut into pieces, perhaps? Jesus, she hoped she wasn't in the company of a psychopathic killer.

Every now and then she could hear steps at the end of the corridor, over the wall of cabinets and desks. They knew there was only one left of them in the building, but it wasn't reassuring to know that it was Riemann, the most powerful of the "non-Euclidean revolutionaries". Academic punks who were playing with the laws of physics, or as they themselves liked to spell it, *physiks*.

While she was still kneeling, she hoped the others would come back soon. Riemann seemed unsettled. More than usual, at least, or more than a non-Euclidean shaper could be. She had seen him in action during the past hours, becoming ever more unpredictable.

They had managed to restrain him with a new biological creation from Charles' capable hands: a curious and deadly mix between an eel and a snake that had chained him to the radiator with its coils. But it was clear that its effect was wearing off. Moreover, this barricade was just an improvised way to barely hide themselves from his powers, and it was becoming thinner and thinner.

It had all started a couple of months before, when Riemann demonstrated his new discoveries in front of the entire maths department in the Aula Magna. He'd started his lecture by opening his bag and pulling out an old leather-bound book: Euclid's *Elements*. He lit up a Bunsen burner that was sitting on his desk and to everyone's disbelief he burned the book. The audience immediately reacted with shock.

"Euclid is dead," Riemann pompously sentenced, chucking what remained of the book into a rubbish bin from which a cloud of ashes soon erupted.

He then wrote on the blackboard until it was fully covered in chalky lines and formulas. Some lines were bending in hyperbolas, other in ellipses. Classical geometry was mocked as old, reactionary and even "sick". Reality obeys whoever describes it, was Riemann's conclusion. And we had been describing reality using Euclid's postulates, so limited and basic, for too long. Childish, even. It was time to start a revolution, a Revolution with a capital R.

"I offer you the new non-Euclidean geometry, the latest and best way to describe reality."

Two parallels never meet, said Euclid in his Fifth Postulate, and continue straight indefinitely without meeting. Riemann's geometry would bend these parallels to resemble hyperbolas and ellipses, thus destroying more than two thousand years of classical geometry. After that lecture, scientists were split between two main parties: the Euclideans and the non-Euclideans. Riemann started to be surrounded by acolytes from all over the world; he became a star in the world of maths and physics, and his face was on all the front pages of the world's newspapers.

"A new era has begun," they read. "Reality is not what it seems"; "Riemann is bending the rules, literally."

2

A sensational popular case, rather unusual for a geometry subject such as that. In the Euclidean party panic spread quite quickly, as their world was crumbling down. Carl Friedrich Gauss' decision to follow Riemann tipped the arguments on the non-Euclidean side further. Departments' funds at universities across the world were slashed in favour of non-Euclidean geometry, Riemann was elected as the president of the National Academy of Sciences, and Gauss even tried to enter politics with some success. The Euclideans were in disarray. A faction fought back and tried to appear in interviews to defend their case. "...both geometries can coexist together. Riemann's geometry can be applied on curved surfaces and Euclidean to flat planes," a prominent physics researcher said in the pages of the *Zeittung*. But conciliatory arguments did not work. The world was ready for the Revolution and Riemann was the new man for a new era.

Then, an obscure Dutch artist by the name of Alfred Escher started to appear at Riemann's right side during every public event. His drawings were rather bizarre and appeared to represent Riemann's geometry somehow, although few non-Euclideans would contest this assertion. Anyway, that was the point of no return for the world. What was until that point just an internal fight for supremacy in the academic world, mocked by some as a childish catfight between boffins, became an open international feudal war and left the realm of academia, with unexpected consequences for all of society.

Riemann started to experiment with reality with his formulas, using what was then dubbed in the tabloids as "dark physiks". With the K, yes. Riemann's tip to the journalist, obviously. He started by bending surfaces, small objects, and later bigger structures like buildings and walls. With his little white chalk he was able to bend reality by simply writing formulas on surfaces. Squared surfaces would become hyperbolic or elliptic, spheres would become pseudospheres and so on, with all the repertoire of exotic names that the non-Euclideans had come up with since its inception. He loved to prove his newly acquired abilities during university lectures, among his peers more than with journalists. He wanted to entertain scientists, not become a

3

magician in a circus. One of these lectures famously finished with the entire audience escaping the building where he was presenting. The blackboard became a sphere (a *pseudosphere*, Gauss corrected the journalists later) and rolled over to the wall. His desk became anisotropic and so too the walls of the hall. It was reported that Riemann was laughing like a madman when all the scientists left the room in panic. Escher was next to him and so was Gauss. Neither of them followed the crowd but stayed put. Riemann had their absolute trust and loyalty.

After surfaces and objects, he then experimented on guinea pigs and mice and he enjoyed their deformities. Biologists protested, but Gauss was able to silence them by simply pushing the government to merge physics and biology faculties together. All of this in a short period of less than six months. The sheer speed of the revolution made some think that there had been a plan since the beginning. A plan to topple the academic institutions as quickly as possible. A non-Euclidean blitzkrieg.

Then one day, the Gottingen Accident struck. Marie was in the first row that day on the university campus, waving her cardboard sign saying, "Stop Riemann destroying our research!" And with her, thousands of other researchers from all branches of science and from all over the world. Riemann was giving a talk at the University of Gottingen and was expecting the usual picketing but this time it was huge. And there was rioting too. Police were unable to keep the crowd outside of the faculty building. Riemann locked himself in the main lecture hall, together with Gauss and Escher and some of the scientists who didn't have time to escape. Witnesses said Riemann was not impressed and calmly reached out to a chest that he had brought into the room earlier that morning. With Gauss' help they removed a machine with a curious shape: a metal post, with a torus or doughnut at the top made of intertwined metal wires. He then wrote a formula with his chalk on the post along its height. Escher wrote something on the wall with his chalk, and on his shoes, and he started to walk on the wall until he reached the ceiling where he squatted like a kid waiting for a ball from the other boys in the street.

4

Gauss started the machine, which was immediately covered in blue sparks. And they waited.

***

Anisotropic shockwaves were spreading in the air like ripples. All matter touched by the ripples deformed like an image on the surface of a pond when a stone is thrown in. Luckily, the shockwaves were too high to be able to touch Marie and the barricade made of furniture absorbed some of them. Cabinets were deforming at the passage of the waves. What was once a perfectly squared quadrilateral with straight and parallel lines became a deformed impossible-to-describe shape. The perversion of geometry was so alien that the human mind couldn't even conceive it, understand it or describe it. Another series of ripples passed very close to her head, such that she felt like she was being pulled by her hair.

"That was close."

Marie spun to see the source of the voice. Erwin had just arrived and was hardly breathing. He looked like he had just finished running a marathon. All sweaty, and his blazer folded and held under his armpit.

"It was about time," Marie said calmly.

"Sorry, but we had some complications along the way. Escher and Gauss are still alive."

"What?"

"Yes, Escher managed to open a channel in the wall, and together with Gauss they escaped through a *forest* of corridors and staircases."

At least all the other non-Euclideans were dead, thought Marie. Or were they? Maybe they just moved to another plane of existence, a plane where two parallels met at last.

Erwin sat next to her and took his rounded glasses away from his face, and cleaned them with a cloth.

"Where is Charles?"

"He is collecting some specimens that we could use against Riemann, but as I mentioned before, I think without you his creations are not going to help us long-term."

Marie rolled her eyes to the ceiling.

5

"I told you before, I can't control it yet on biological matter."

"But Marie, it is all getting out of hand, if you haven't noticed. The government and the army are trusting us. You said to the police chief that this should have been fought internally between us scientists, before the police or the army could intervene."

"Yes, but I need to find the right way and time to channel it. I killed my husband with my own hands, Erwin, for God's sake!"

Erwin stepped back and put his hands up in the air, avoiding her gaze.

"I know, sorry."

And in that moment Riemann's voice was heard, screaming and grizzling.

"You fucking Euclideans! I will destroy you once and for all!"

Erwin and Marie looked at each other, fear in their faces. The eel-snake was losing strength and stopped trying to bite him. It was coiling around the radiator many times, but you could see the knot of flesh and scales becoming looser and looser. Its upper body was coiled around Riemann's arm and its head, once ferocious and deadly, was now deformed. Its jaws were split in an elliptic fashion, one of the anisotropic shockwaves from Riemann had damaged it for good. It was a miracle it was still alive.

"He is unstable," Erwin said.

"What do you mean?"

"Look at his forehead."

Marie popped her head up for few seconds and saw Riemann's twitching like he was in seizures. His teeth were continuously grinding against each other like he had sand in his molars. At one point he was holding his head like he couldn't contain its contents anymore, and it was in that moment that another shockwave originated from his head. Marie ducked just in time to avoid the ripples in the air but she saw what Erwin was talking about: his forehead was scarred with blood.

"He wrote a non-Euclidean formula on himself! He made himself anisotropic!"

6

"That's why he is bursting with shockwaves. He can't contain them any longer. He will have bigger and more powerful bursts until..."

"Until?"

"Until he might end up with one final burst."

"And then?"

"And then it could be the end of the world as we know it, Marie."

"A singularity."

"Not a simple singularity: a Riemann's singularity, that could wipe out the universe as we know it. It could rewrite the laws of physics and base it on its new, perverse geometry."

Riemann erupted in anger again and again, swearing and cursing at them repeatedly. He could hear some of their conversation, as only a few metres of desks and chairs were separating them from him. The shockwaves stopped when he was shouting, which was a good sign. Maybe it was good to let him discharge all his anger towards them. Erwin had an idea.

"Bernhard Riemann, it's over. Gauss and Escher are dead."

Marie widened her eyes when she heard that bluff.

"All your acolytes are dead. You are the last one and I know what you have done to yourself."

"You know nothing, you Austrian prick!"

"How do you think it is going to end up, Riemann?"

"With you, all of you, dead! And with the fabric of space finally hyperbolic."

"Whatever. But you will die too."

Raucous laughter was the reply.

Then there was silence. Erwin and Marie looked at each other. Erwin checked over the barricade and saw him in a foetal position, holding his head like a baby. It seemed that letting him shout and swear had worked out pretty well. It was like the shockwaves were a physical representation of his anger. The eel-snake was now dead and hanging from his arm.

Erwin told Marie and they both relaxed, for now.

"How was my box? Did you take care of it?"

"Ah, talking about that. There is a horrible smell coming out of there. What are you hiding in it?"

Erwin smiled and touched the wooden box like it was his girlfriend.

"You will see."

"I have a bad feeling about it. You know, there is something in there, alive I mean, but yet it smells of death."

"You got the point. I think Charles will be able to help a little with it."

She didn't get what he meant, but mentioning Charles let her mind think about him. They started to worry about Charles. Erwin had left him behind more than an hour ago. With Gauss and Escher still on the run, there was danger coming from everywhere. Escher was able to pierce through walls and buildings, and to create warped tunnels and staircases that went everywhere and nowhere at the same time. He was the artist of the group: he did not only perverted geometry, he perverted beauty and feelings.

And then they saw Charles running towards them holding a sack, like an out-of-season Santa Claus. His long, white beard flowing back over his shoulder.

"Here I am, I brought some presents for Riemann."

"Charles Darwin, you do look like Santa indeed. Hope that was a conscious pun," Marie said with a sarcastic grin.

Charles looked at Marie and then to Erwin. He put down the sack and something inside was moving furiously. He ignored it and continued to look at Marie.

"Marie Curie, I think it's time to channel your powers once and for all."

He opened the sack and took hold of a leash. A dog, a golden retriever, jumped out of it and hid behind Charles's legs.

"With your help we can make wonders with this."

Marie looked Erwin in the eyes, then held her head above the barricade, Riemann not being a danger for the moment. Pierre came immediately to her mind, a sad face corroded by radiation. Radiation that emanated from her, from her hands. She still remembered the smell coming from them. Burned skin, smoky flavours, at times like holy frankincense. She couldn't forget that smell and she knew that smelling it again would make her beg for death. Being

8

the murderer of your own husband, the second-half of yourself; it was a burden that would never leave her shoulders. Homicide, although she pleaded innocent in front of the judge. Only Erwin and Charles knew about it, and only a partial truth. She never went to prison but the everyday thought of him was jail enough. Since then she used her powers only once, by accident in Charles's lab. And what came out was an extraordinary surprise. She could combine her powers with those of others. But soon came the realisation that she couldn't control them, and she didn't want to kill anyone else, anymore. She promised herself that her hands would not become as red as lava anymore, that her hands would not spark powerful and deadly X-rays anymore against any living creature.

But then she looked at that maniac against the radiator, momentarily powerless but potentially deadly again. She thought of all the scientists, PhDs, postdocs, assistants, professors, junior and senior researchers, technicians, even some secretaries who had lost their lives in the nonsense battle of those days. Hundreds of lives, both Euclidean and non, gone because of the madness of a raving maniac. Perhaps using her powers another time, the last time, would finish all the pain inflicted on this world. Perhaps she needed to do it for Pierre. It was time to finish it. It was time to kill Riemann once and for all.

She nodded to the air, her eyes cast down, her skin pale as death. She was ready to die again. This time to save lives. This time for the sake of humanity.

Charles understood and pulled the dog into the middle, between them. Signed with his head for Erwin to move away. Erwin put ten metres between him and them, reaching the far end of the corridor, not knowing yet that what he was going to see that day, from there, he would never forget.

Charles kept the dog calm between him and Marie, petting it on the head. The dog seemed to stop shivering and started to wag its tail timidly. He then took off his long jacket and put both of his hands on the animal's head, like he was going to kiss it any minute. He closed his eyes and pulled his head back as if in a trance. For few minutes there was silence, then the dog whined a little, and then more and more until it reached a peak that was unmistakably close to pain. Something happened to it the moment it stopped whining. A bulge started to appear at the base of its neck, the fur swelling. Almost like a tumour. A tumour that moved. Something was moving underneath the dog's skin. Something big erupted from it and it wasn't pretty at all. First a burst of blood, then white bone, after that red tissue like flesh started to grow from beneath the fur and wrapped around the bones. On top of the vertebrae that formed, a blob of white matter, and then flesh started to conglomerate and a skull was made. Eye bulbs formed, and then teeth grew and ears and muscles all over the face. Skin and hair were the last to appear. The same thing was repeated on the other side of its neck, but by this time Erwin was in a state of shock and could not remember the second head coming out. In all of this the dog stayed still and Charles didn't open his eyes, not even once. Marie's face was turned to the barricade and a hand was at her mouth like she was ready to throw up. A Cerberus was born from the hands of Charles Darwin. A Cerberus that wagged its tail and licked his hands like a puppy. Actually, like three puppies. The heads were at first uncoordinated and were banging against each other. One head, the original one, started to bite the others, but soon realised it was no match for the other two. It calmed down after a while.

Then Charles get go and tied the leash to a desk. He crawled away from the scene towards Erwin and lay on the floor, exhausted, metres away. Erwin did not go to help him or ask anything. He knew it was painful, but temporarily for him.

When Marie placed her hands on the three-headed dog, lights in the building faded down. All went dark. This time all three dog heads were whining, not just the original one. Erwin was the reluctant spectator of that freak show. First the creation of a mythical beast, then the beginning of a second ritual in complete darkness. A few metres away a maniac was bound to a radiator by a dying eel-snake chain monster. Erwin's heart was pounding and his mind was losing its way.

From the pitch dark a gentle glow appeared. It was coming from Marie's hands. It was as if she was holding a globe of fluorescent matter, like a fairy epiphany. The dog(s) stopped whining and looked at her hands, which were now illuminating enough to show Marie's face and the three-headed dog's noses. Her hands became gradually brighter and brighter until they reached an intense red colour like lava, whiter in the centres of her palms, while the colour spectrum changed from yellow to red the farther it moved from the centre.

Erwin started to smell something smoky in the air. Burned meat and cinnamon, and a hint of rotten fish, a strange and unappealing mix of odours. He saw her touching the dogs' heads one by one and he could distinctively hear their fur burning. When she removed her hands there were marks on the heads, then the body of the poor animal started to boil. Literally boiling underneath the skin and hairs. Its shape was everchanging and bubbles of flesh were coming up to the surface. Erwin was so tense that he didn't realise Charles was standing next to him now. He was searching for something inside his little bag. He took a glass vial in his hand containing something brightly coloured, and quickly tossed it towards the blob that was a three-headed dog. Charles would then have told him it was a live hornet. "Just to spice it up," Charles justified to himself, smiling.

The blob grew and grew until it reached a height of a metre or so. It then gradually calmed down and took the shape of a much bigger dog with ferocious fangs and extremely aggressive behaviour. The collar wasn't able to contain its main neck and snapped, leaving it unleashed. Charles moved forward somewhat, knowing how to calm the beast. Erwin dashed towards Marie, who was lying on the pavement unconscious.

"Do not touch her hands!" Charles shouted. "She will be fine. Keep your distance for a few more minutes. Otherwise you will end up like her husband."

Erwin stopped mid-way and didn't know what to do. To his right there was an old, bearded Englishman trying to calm down a three-headed mythical beast. To his left, a multi-awarded Nobel laureate lady, now unconscious and with deadly hands like furnaces. What a time to live in.

# Chapter 2
## The Accident

The Gottingen Accident made them all. It made them like this. Superhumans. Or supermonsters, depending on what you thought of their powers. And it was all thanks to, or because of, Riemann. When the rioting crowd reached the hall where he was giving his lecture in Gottingen a huge burst of sparks erupted from its wooden door. It reached the outermost corners of the faculty, hitting all the people on its way. Most of the researchers died, but what Riemann couldn't know was that the devastating power of his machine could give death to most, but grant new life to a few.

Ivan Pavlov could evoke conditioned reflexes on any living being. He hadn't had enough time to experiment on humans when he was arrested in Russia by the Soviet secret service and forcibly enrolled in a military programme to condition soldiers.

Dmitri Mendeleev was hospitalised for months with symptoms of hypersomnia. When he woke up, he filled his table with thirty-five new more elements.

Konrad Lorenz gained the ability to communicate with any creature in the animal kingdom. He set foot in a zoo only once, then he locked himself in an apartment for the rest of his life. We will never know what the animals said to him.

Albert Einstein gave birth to a twin from his hip. An identical twin that in a matter of hours grew as big as him. It was a relativity twin. The farther he was from Einstein, the older he became. They ended up living next to each other all the time like Siamese twins.

James Maxwell was punished by the appearance at his side of a little demon, who never disappeared from his shoulder and made all sorts of jokes.

But not all the researchers gained extravagant or disturbing powers. Some were gifted with powers that were more useful. Marie Curie gained the power to use the same X-rays she had discovered alongside her husband. She could direct the rays with her hands and see through objects.

Charles Darwin could modify any biological structure to his will, bypassing natural selection.

There were also scientists who were consumed by their powers. Max Planck simply vanished in what people called a "quantum leap". Some of his admirers thought he was still alive, but in a quantum state. Enrico Fermi gained the ability to split atoms, something that didn't end up well when he experimented on transuranic elements. Ludwig Boltzmann disappeared in a cloud of gases and was never to be found again.

Even Escher was hit by it, and that granted him the powers he was enjoying so much now: opening doors to his non-Euclidean world of imagination with staircases and doors.

Everyone knew that Gauss was hit too, but so far he didn't show any newly acquired powers. And that was something to be afraid of. Maybe he was keeping them until the end, Marie thought.

Apart from Fermi, who died in a mini-nuclear explosion, Marie Curie was by far the most powerful of them all. So powerful that her powers were consuming her day by day. Every time she used them she felt weaker and weaker. It took longer and longer to recover from each burst of X-ray usage. The first time she realised about her powers she was still in bed in her apartment, two days after the accident. Pierre wasn't in bed next to her. She could hear him cooking something for lunch in the kitchen. Apparently, she had remained unconscious for two solid days. She could hardly remember what happened. There was a flash, then blue sparks all over the corridor where the rioters were

13

assembled. The wooden door that separated them from Riemann was in pieces, destroyed by the flashy blast. She could not recall any sound or voice from that moment. It was as if her ears were gone. She had some memories (but they could be false memories) of people's faces around her in panic, mouths open, screaming in pain. No one that she could recognise though. Later she was informed that most of those faces belonged to researchers who were now dead. She was one of the few survivors of the blast. Pierre was still moving cutlery and pans in the kitchen. She didn't want to interrupt him. She tried to lift herself up, helping with her elbows on the mattress. It was painful and her bones were aching all over. Her mouth was dry too, but she found a glass full of water next to her bed. Someone, Pierre, had been taking care of her all the time. The light was very dim, curtains were drawn and she could barely see the sunlight coming through the shutters on the window in front of her. The light was enough, though, to let her see what had happened to the bedsheets. They were all charred at her hip level. Little by little, she realised that the charred shapes resembled hands. Her hands.

Had she smoked while she was sleeping and the sheets had got burned? She had sleepwalked in the past, but this was a different level of sleepwalking. Maybe an ashtray fell while she was sleeping?

"What the hell..." she whispered, loud enough for Pierre to notice that she was awake.

Pierre came in the room quickly.

"Sweetheart, you are awake at last!"

"Pierre, what happened?" she asked, while he hugged her gently and kissed her neck.

"You were unconscious for two days. At first the doctor thought you were in a coma, but that was clearly not the case as you were talking and responding to stimuli during your sleep. You just needed a good restoring sleep, that's all."

"But what..." She could not find the words.

"There in Gottingen? It's in all the newspapers. Riemann used a sort of weapon that hit all of you. Sadly, most of your colleagues didn't make it, but you were miraculously spared."

14

He hugged her again and tears started to fall from his cheeks.

"That criminal. I can't believe what he did."

"An arrest warrant has been issued. Right now he is on the run, together with those creepy acolytes of his."

Marie stayed speechless.

"But don't worry, they are going to arrest him. Even the army has been dispatched. He can't be far from Gottingen."

"Who survived?"

"A handful of scientists. I know of Charles Darwin and Konrad Lorenz because they came to visit you whilst you were asleep. For them the shock was smaller, as they were far away from the blast."

Marie moved her gaze to the charred, hand-shaped stains.

"Oh, about that," Pierre said. "Last night you had a high fever and... you did that."

"What is it?"

"Your hands were burning, first red than white as phosphorus. They fluoresced for minutes. Hence those marks on the sheets."

Marie could not believe what she was hearing. She brought her hands close to her face and inspected them. They looked normal, normal as always. Maybe a bit pale, but after what had happened what could you expect?

"The first night was similar but you didn't manage to burn the sheets. The doctor was shocked. We immediately linked it to the accident at the university. But it's currently unexplainable."

The following days seemed like normal days in Curie's house. Marie recovered from the accident and her hands never turned red and hot like the first two nights. One day, Pierre came back home and said: "I've met Charles on the university campus. He said he would love to pass by this afternoon for a tea."

"Sure, no problem."

"I thought he could give us more insight into what has happened there, and perhaps explain... you."

"Sure," Marie said, in a way that almost made her forget about her hands. "I'll prepare a cake for this afternoon," she said timidly.

15

Charles arrived at four sharp. Pierre invited him into the kitchen, where Marie had just finished garnishing the cake. He was using a stick and was limping quite badly. His old age and the accident didn't fare well on his body. After shaking hands and a bit of small talk, he asked if they could sit.

"I'm so tired lately. I've passed the past few nights with hardly any sleep."

Marie and Pierre sat at the table next to him.

"Sorry to hear that."

"But I'm happy to see you, Marie. I mean, still with us."

He grasped one of her hands and she felt a burning emanating from her skin. She retracted her hand quickly, as if stung by a needle. Charles didn't seem to notice it.

"The fate of many others was not that clement. We are lucky, Marie, to still be alive," he said, looking her in the eyes.

"I lost contact with some of the others who survived. Pavlov and Mendeleev went back to Russia. But I know that Einstein, Maxwell and Lorenz are still around. I meet with them every now and then. We have been interviewed by all the international newspapers. We became more famous because of this accident than for our research. It is sad, really. Months and months on the *Beagle* collecting specimens, and no one from the press cared about me. At least you got your Nobel prizes but I can assure you the public looks at us in a different way now. We are celebrities. You should go out more often, Marie, and enjoy it while it lasts."

"I'm not that kind of person, you know me."

Pierre stopped the conversation to dispel the tension.

"Would you like tea and cake, Charles?"

"I would love to."

Teacups were placed on the table.

"Any milk?" asked Charles.

"No, we don't have any."

"I'm afraid I can't have my tea without milk."

Pierre had forgotten about the British habit of drinking tea with milk, and Charles seemed to have quite a strong opinion about it.

16

"I'm going to buy some from the grocers down the road. Just give me ten minutes."

And Pierre was gone. When Charles turned his face to Marie after the door shut, Marie understood that it was his plan all along to get rid of Pierre from the room.

He leaned on the table towards her, his long white beard touching the cake.

"Marie, have you felt anything... weird recently? Something unusual? There are rumours of the others who survived, of peculiar... how can I describe it? Peculiar powers, so to speak."

She shook her head vigorously and said no repeatedly. He sat back in his chair and sighed in relief.

"Good for you, Marie."

There was silence. Marie sipped from her cup and offered some cake. Then he leaned forward again, and almost whispered: "Because I gained something that day."

He then started to describe his newly acquired powers. He found out about them when he was taking care of the finches he had brought back from his voyage to the Galapagos. He took one from the cage and gently put it in another, as he needed to clean the bird's mess. While holding it he went into a sort of trance. When he awoke from it, the finch had a longer beak. Much longer. Over the next couple of days it happened again, with other finches. Longer or thicker beaks, longer wings, or feathers with different colours. He understood he could control it by concentrating his mind on the wanted phenotype. He could shape life as he pleased. Without waiting for natural selection to do its bidding.

Marie listened in silence. Of course, she couldn't believe what he was saying. Was he mad? The blast made him more demented than an old man of his age should be.

"You don't believe me, right?"

He took a vial from his blazer's inside pocket. There was a fly in there, alive. He took it out pinching its wings with his fingers and showed it to her. It was buzzing and trying to escape from his fingertips.

"Behold."

His head went back, as if his hair was pulled from behind by an invisible hand. His eyelids closed, his lips

17

tightly glued to each other. She was concentrating so hard on his face that she didn't realise something was happening to the fly for real. The transparent wings filled with black liquid through the veins on the surface. Then they grew, as the black liquid pumped in matter. They grew four times in length, and they resembled those of a dragonfly now. The black ink was sucked out of the membranous wings and they returned to being transparent. When he set the fly free, it was unable to fly anymore. It just dropped on the table, trying to move its wings, but was only able to drag them while walking on its tiny legs.

"Do you believe me now?" he asked, biting into the cake. Crumbs fell all over his beard.

"I'm back." Pierre's voice came from the main door.

Charles immediately took the fly and put it back in the vial and in his pocket.

"Hope the tea is not cold now," Pierre said, coming in through the kitchen door.

They had tea and they spoke about Riemann and Gauss. Marie didn't feel well after what she had seen with the fly. Her mind was still trying to process what she saw. Did she really see the fly's wings growing disproportionally? She wanted to ask Charles to show it to Pierre too, so she couldn't be called crazy, but she refrained. Charles wanted only her to see it, as was obvious from the fact that he had sent Pierre to buy milk and hid the fly when he was back. She wanted to wash her face with cold water.

"If you'll excuse me."

She went to the bathroom and washed her face. She looked at her image in the mirror for several long minutes, trying to read something in her newly formed wrinkles. First Riemann's powers, then the accident, her hot and burning hands, now Charles's powers and that prodigy that unfolded in front of her eyes. What the hell was going on?

She needed to go back to the kitchen before someone realised that she wasn't right. She straightened the mirror as she always did before exiting the bathroom. She had told Pierre to put another nail in the wall so many times that... was it a fluorescent shape that she saw on the wall? She stopped and squeezed her eyes tight, to focus on where she saw an evanescent shape moving in the wall.

18

Nothing. She must have had a hallucination. After all that had happened in recent days. She stepped towards the door when again she saw something moving on the wall, like a bright shadow. Then she understood that the closer her body was to the wall, the more often she could see those shapes. She put her palms on the wall and she saw them. Fluorescent human silhouettes moving back and forth on the wall's surface. Two, to be precise. And they were skeletons, for sure. She had seen those shapes before. She had seen those bones before. In her radiographies. And those were her neighbours, Ann and Thomas, walking in their lounge on the other side of the wall, over the wall. *Through the wall!*

Ten minutes later, when Charles and Pierre forced the bathroom door and found the pale and comatose body of Marie on the floor, Charles could see the charred shapes of two hands on the wallpaper.

## Chapter 3
## The Escherian Portal

When Marie awoke a few minutes after her monstrous experiment on the three-headed dog, her hands were already back to normal. Apart from that particular smell still in the corridor, nothing suggested that she had been through that transformation. Except the beast she had created, of course. Charles had managed to tame it, but the heads were still fighting with each other. He was trying to stay away from their fangs. "They might have venom. You know, from the hornet I threw in earlier," he said to Erwin. He even tried to teach it to sit. "Sit!" he was shouting, pointing to the floor. But when the main (original) head listened to him and tried to command the body to sit, the other two heads distracted it and it started again from scratch.

Erwin asked himself how on earth anyone could tame such a creature. Teach it how to roll? Play dead? Return a stick? He hoped they had summoned the right tool to kill Riemann.

Right, Riemann. What was he up to?

He was asking himself that question when they heard another shockwave, but this time with a different tone, as if it was coming from a different source. No ripples in reality like before. Where Riemann was squatting like a child in despair, now there was an opening, like a window that let them see through the wall and the floor: an impossible,

20

intricate jungle of staircases and steps leading to everywhere and nowhere, and doors opening up, down, upside-down. Going up and down, back and forth on this maze of stairs were Escher and Gauss, holding Riemann by his armpits, unconscious. They appeared and disappeared through different doors. It was chaotic, unsettling, and Charles wanted to throw up from the absence of real coordinates. The passage stayed open, unlike the other times they had seen Escher going through his drawings and then closing the passage behind him.

"He must have forgotten to close this one. We can follow them now."

"Follow them there? Are you crazy?" Marie said, forcing herself to her feet. "We will get stripped apart by the non-Euclidean geometry. Our minds will get warped in those jungles of geometric impossibilities."

"Perhaps, or perhaps not. We can test it by asking Newton to step in first."

"Newton? Now you are giving that thing a name? Newton?" asked Marie.

"That was the name written on its collar. It must have been a physicist's dog. That's why I found it wandering in the faculty gardens."

"Jesus, poor Isaac."

They moved some of the furniture, enough to create a passage for both Newton and them. The beast seemed to calm down when it focused its attention on the non-Euclidean wall aperture. All three heads barked at it. And more, and more and more. It was like the convoluted staircases were mesmerising the creature, which kept being drawn to the portal.

"What's the matter, Newton?"

Charles was treating the beast like a puppy.

*Sure, now he's going to tell it, "Who's a good boy? Yes, you are!"* Marie thought, shaking her head slowly.

"We have to restrain Newton before he jumps in and we lose him."

He dashed quickly – *How can an old man like him be so athletic? He could barely stand in my kitchen after the accident*, thought Marie – to the opposite wall and broke the glass of the fire hydrant. He pulled the hose out and unscrewed the end that kept it attached to the main valve. After he made a knot around Newton's central neck, he secured it to his waist with another knot.

"That's a tad thoughtless," Erwin said, and just when he'd finished saying it Newton jumped through Escher's portal, dragging metres and metres of hose with it. Charles realised too late how stupid he had been. The hose strengthened until the tension reached a peak and Charles started to be dragged towards the non-Euclidean portal. He immediately tried to pull the hose with his hands, but Newton was pulling and pulling. Pulling so much that the knot around Charles's waist was becoming tighter and tighter. It was now impossible to loosen it.

Erwin and Marie jumped to his aid and pulled him by his coat, but all three were being dragged inside now. Erwin understood that the only way was to cut the hose. He let go his hold on the coat and jumped into the barricade. He had to find something sharp.

"Erwin, where are you going? Don't leave us alone!" Marie was shouting without understanding Erwin's plan.

She looked at the wall aperture and couldn't believe her eyes. The hose, straight like a pole from Charles's waist up to the wall, started to deform within the aperture. Curving and then zigzagging and then curving again, suspended in the air. Nevertheless, it was pulling in a straight fashion, defying all the laws of physics. Euclidean physics, at least. Newton was running up and down the stairs, disappearing from a staircase that was climbing up and appearing upside-down from a door tens of metres away. Its heads popped in through a door but its tail was sticking out from another one several metres away and oriented in different directions. That place was the creation of pure madness.

Marie stopped looking at the "painting" on the wall, because she was starting to feel sick just by looking at it. She focused on Charles more and more. He was risking being dragged into the painting and… who knows what was going to happen to him. And Erwin had disappeared over the barricade and she couldn't see him anymore. Did he abandon them? Not surprising, though. He had always been a weird character. She would never forget the first time she met him, a few days after the Gottingen Accident. Charles

22

had just revealed his superpowers and she had just discovered she could see through walls and people. Erwin wasn't part of the crowd that was hit by the waves in Gottingen.

"I was on my sabbatical," he said, while sitting in the last row of the theatre where all the survivors of the accident met for the first time. He was the only one in that theatre who wasn't present that day, and people wondered why he was there. Was he just curious or, as some people thought, a bit jealous that he hadn't acquired any powers?

That day it was like an Alcoholics Anonymous meeting. Marie was the third to jump up onto the stage, the red curtains just slightly open at her back.

"I am Dr Marie Curie and I can burn stuff with my hands... and see through walls like in a radiograph."

The small crowd murmured in awe. The previous two scientists who had described their powers were disappointing. Their powers were very weak and without any real use in everyday life.

"I found out about my powers right after the accident, when I burned my bedsheets with my hands without noticing it. I'm much better now at controlling it, so do not worry."

Someone in the theatre laughed; that was Erwin, at the back. He sat isolated from the others, five or six empty rows apart from the rest.

That night others followed, including Charles Darwin and Konrad Lorenz, who brought a chicken with him to demonstrate how he could talk with animals. Unfortunately, the chicken that night didn't want to say anything apart from the usual request for food. Konrad was very disappointed and left the theatre immediately after his failed demonstration. Apparently, he discovered later, some animals can be as shy in front of crowds as humans. People that night believed him, though. Although his powers were nothing compared to Marie's or Charles's.

Charles brought a mouse and made its neck elongate, its ears shrink and its paws develop two additional fingers. The crowd was in a mixture of shock and awe. Then someone suggested to him that he should stop with the

23

awkward mutations. Later, rumours spread of an old lady that threw up her dinner in the public toilets.

Erwin didn't jump onto the stage but sat listening, with his mouth always open in amazement and ready to clap at the end of each demonstration. He then approached Marie when the "freak show", as Marie herself thought of it, was over.

"Marie Curie?"

"Yes."

"Hi, my name is Erwin. I'm a physicist. I work at the Gottingen University but I wasn't there for the accident."

"Lucky you."

"Well, judging by your powers I wish I could have been there with you."

"We are the survivors. You probably didn't notice that everyone else is dead. We were in our thousands there; today, we barely filled a third of a one-hundred-capacity theatre."

Erwin ducked his head and touched his rounded glasses, showing shame.

"Sorry, I didn't mean to..."

"I know, no worries. What can I do for you?"

Erwin couldn't talk and left his mouth open. Marie looked at him for a while, then she waved goodbye to her fellow scientists who were leaving the theatre.

"Did you enjoy it today?" she asked to break the ice.

"Yes, very much. I think your powers are by far the best and most powerful. What are you planning to use them for?"

And that question hit her like a bullet. She had discovered her powers weeks ago, but she had never thought about that. What was she going to use her powers for? She thought they were a curse, or at least a freakish burden. A handicap more than a gift. This man that she had just met was suggesting to her that she could use them for something.

"Are they of any use?" she asked.

"Well, sure, of course. You can see through walls!"

"Apart from spying on my neighbours and seeing their skeletons, I can't see any good in them."

24

"But you need to think big. You know, even Superman can do the same but he doesn't spend his time peeping at others' houses, like a pervert."

Marie widened her eyes immediately.

"Uh, I didn't mean to say you were a pervert. Sorry!"

"Of course you didn't."

Erwin reached into an internal pocket in his long coat and took out a comic book. The cover depicted Superman firing laser beams from his eyes at a generic villain, while flying between skyscrapers.

"Maybe you can be like him. Ah, there is Supergirl as well," he added while showing it to her.

"I'm afraid it's not my style," she said, looking at the door where she saw Pierre waving to her.

"I have to go now. My husband is waiting at the door. It was nice meeting you though."

Erwin's face was showily disappointed when he heard the word *husband*. Marie noticed it but pretended she hadn't. She waved briefly at him and ran towards Pierre. She kissed him and they quickly went out of the theatre. Marie felt a hand on her elbow, and when she spun she saw Erwin handing her the comic book.

"You can use your powers for better uses, Marie. I'm sure you can do great things with them."

She took the comic book and remained speechless.

"Perhaps I'll see you again."

And he stood at the main door of the theatre, cleaning his rounded glasses, while Marie and Pierre returned to their car.

\*\*\*

Erwin was standing next to Charles again when Marie looked away from the painting. He was trying to cut the hose with a sharp piece of glass. Probably from one of the cabinets in the barricade. He hadn't abandoned them in the end. They all fell to the ground when Newton turned a corner and tugged the hose. Erwin worked hard and quickly on the hose, but the fabric was very difficult to cut. He finally managed to break through by using a sharp triangular tip as a stiletto. Charles saw the opportunity to pull it and the fabric gave up. Charles backlashed on the ground and the hose was unleashed, and so was Newton inside Escher's world. Last time they saw it, it was howling, times three, and running up stairs that were going down. And then it disappeared.

There was silence for almost a minute. Charles banged his head on the floor and was breathing loudly. Erwin dropped his glasses and was all sweaty. Marie was trying to recover her strength after all that action.

"What do we do now?" Charles asked, still staring at the ceiling.

"I guess we inform the police that we failed and that it is now their problem," Erwin said in a very dismissive way.

"No way. We've come to this point and now we give up? It's now a personal fight between us and Riemann," Marie said, standing with clutched fists.

"She is right, Erwin," Charles said, pulling himself up and trying to unknot the hose still around his waist. "Despite everything, Newton survived in there, without giving up his Euclidean form. It shouldn't affect our bodies and it's the only way forward to reach to Riemann. Police, or even the army, are powerless against him."

"So are we. We've lost our weapon of choice and now it is howling in there, lost forever."

"Ariadne's thread," whispered Charles.

"What?"

"You are right. We are going to get lost in there unless we use a thread that can still bind us to the classical reality. That's a maze. And Newton just got lost in it."

"This time longer than that bloody hose reel, I hope," Marie said, nodding.

"Let's go and talk to the army general you spoke to earlier, Marie. They might have a longer cable we can attach it to."

Earlier that day, Marie had had a very fiery conversation with both a police chief and an army general in the gardens of the main campus. They'd wanted to intervene against Riemann, of course, as he had become a threat to national security. After the Gottingen Accident he was the most wanted man in Europe. He disappeared in the aftermath, together with Escher and Gauss, but

26

resurfaced in various locations in Europe. Mostly universities and physics departments. They suspected he was using the portals that Escher was able to open in the walls. These portals could open anywhere and could lead anywhere. It was impossible to predict where they would have resurfaced once they got in. It wasn't clear why they were popping up in the real world only in universities. There was no pattern, but many thefts of machines and mechanical tools were reported in all the physics departments they sneaked into.

The police chief who Marie talked to that day thought they were collecting parts to build an even bigger weapon, beside which the one in Gottingen was nothing in comparison. That's why the army was summoned immediately. A tank was facing its cannon towards the institute in Gottingen were Riemann had been spotted a few hours before. Somehow, Riemann had come back to the same place where it all started. Marie, together with Charles, had asked him politely to let them intervene.

"We know how to stop him," she bluffed.

"I'm sorry Dr Curie, but this has become a case of national security. That man is dangerous."

"I bloody know it myself, he used his weapon on me."

Schmidtz, the police chief, had a huge, pointy moustache and a shiny helmet on his rather little head. He was one of the medal-appointed heroes who had won the Great War a few years earlier. He'd served on the French front. After the German victory he could have taken advantage of an early retirement, but he chose to serve in the police instead. He was a staunch monarchist and thought his experiences during the war could have been better used in the *anti-revolutionary* police, a special wing of the police that was formed after the failed October 1917 Bolshevik revolution in Russia. It became necessary when the tsar expelled all the opposition and most of the "communist scum", as Schmidtz liked to call them, escaped to western Europe. In Spain, where many of the Bolsheviks fled, a civil war was tipping towards them. The Kaiser didn't want that to happen in Germany. The situation was relatively calm and small groups were constantly monitored. And that's why he was summoned to Gottingen to stop

27

Riemann. Initial reports led them to think it was a very active Bolshevik group that detonated that dirty bomb.

"I know what happened to you... scientists that day. But that's not a good excuse to vindicate a crime personally."

"It's not about personal vengeance, Chief. Well, not only. We are his peers, we know his weaknesses and we know a bit of non-Euclidean geometry. Enough not to get killed like *his* stupid soldiers early on," she said, pointing at the army general who was standing next to them in silence.

The army general had just lost a battalion of forty-five men that he sent towards Riemann. He didn't know that Riemann had previously written non-Euclidean equations on the floor of the main hall where his men first entered the building. The floor became an elliptic surface, trapping them like in a gigantic bowl. Then it squashed them like ants when its surfaces became hyperbolic. The tank didn't fare better, as the projectiles' trajectories were bent by Riemann's perverted geometry and came back to their sender. It was a disaster. They were fighting against an alien physics. Their weapons were made for this world, not for Riemann's.

"Give us a chance to show we can stop him."

"I'm afraid I can't, Dr Curie."

"Marie, leave it like this," Charles said, gently touching her shoulder.

She wasn't a woman who could give up that easily. She went past the police chief and the army general until she reached the head of the tank with her hands. After a minute of concentration, her hands were visibly becoming red like magma. The steel of the tank started to change colour too, but it was only when the men inside started to escape quickly and shout from the tank turret followed by a smoky cloud that everyone realised the effect she'd had on the tank. That small lady had the power to effectively stop a tank without destroying it.

"She has balls," commented the army general without looking at her. He then talked to the police chief in private for a couple of never-ending minutes. The soldiers who manned the tank were now calmer and described the horrible sensations they had experienced and the short-circuited console that had caught fire.

"I guess we can give you a couple of hours to try to capture him, dead or alive. Then, if you fail, we bomb the department to the ground. We can't afford to let him escape again," Schmidtz said in a whisper, so the others couldn't listen.

Marie didn't waste her time and she grabbed Charles's arm. They ran towards the physics department as fast as they could.

"What did he say to you?"

"He said be quick or be dead."

"What?"

"If we fail, they will bomb the shit out of us."

The building was at the end of a big lawn that they needed to cross. They had crossed half the distance when they heard someone shouting from where the army was standing. They turned and saw a man in his mid-thirties with rounded glasses trying to pass through the armed soldiers. He was shouting towards them.

"That's Erwin. He made it then!" said Charles.

"Who?"

"He's with us. Let him pass," Charles yelled at the soldiers.

The general gave the order to let him pass and Erwin ran towards them. On his back he was carrying a big wooden box or crate. He was holding it like a backpack with ropes as straps.

"Hi Charles, thanks."

"No problem. You made it in the end."

"Yes, I managed to pass through the first security cordon but not this one. Luckily I saw you walking towards the building."

"Erwin, this is Dr Marie Curie."

"Yeah, we know each other already," Erwin said with a smile.

Marie then realised who he was. That weird man in the theatre weeks ago. The one who gave her the Superman comic.

"Hi Erwin. How are you doing?"

"Not too bad thanks."

29

"I still have your comic."

"Yes, keep it, no problem. I've got loads of them at home."

"Comic?" asked Charles "Never mind, we have to go. Marie, I invited Erwin because I think he can be of great help in defeating Riemann. He is a physicist with a lot of experience on quantum theory."

"So, what's the situation?" Erwin asked.

"We have a maniac on the run who wants to destroy or rule the world, or both," Marie said, walking quickly through the main doors of the faculty building.

Charles gave more useful details.

"Riemann and his acolytes resurfaced in Gottingen yesterday. The army sent several men and tanks, but it didn't work out well. There will be no coffins to fill up for the families."

And when he finished saying that last sentence he pointed at the floor of the main hall. Erwin stopped. What he saw was shocking: the rectangular marble tiles of the floor were scattered across the air. Literally floating in the air. It was hard to describe it, but it was like there was a huge pit in the ground shaped as a bowl, but lines were following weird and impossible paths. The tiles were floating over this pit in a specific pattern that Charles described as hyperbolic. It was non-Euclidean geometry at its weirdest. He could see military uniforms and rifles spread all over, but no bodies.

"Bodies would have been squashed to nothing when the floor collapsed and then folded onto them. They will hardly find any remains," Charles said with a hieratic tone.

"We have to pass through the canteen. We know that Riemann and the others are in the west wing," Marie said, leading the way.

The others followed her through a side door that opened into a long corridor. They followed it until it turned left, then they suddenly stopped. The rest of the corridor was a jungle of non-Euclidean geometries. Walls were not parallel in this corridor and they were bending, sometimes inwards, others outwards. Passing through it was nevertheless a "straight" experience as although their brains were telling them something, their walking experience was telling them something else.

The doors were curved almost like spheres, but they opened normally. Ceiling and floor were anamorphic, almost like those street artists who paint a scene on the pavement of a square that can only be seen by looking from a certain point of view. Three-dimensional projections were continuously changing depending on the point of view of the observer. Other objects were floating in the air like they were bound to the invisible wires of a puppeteer.

It was sensorial madness, and Charles took the lead now.

"Do not look at the walls and the ceiling and the floor. Just fix on a point at the end of the corridor and stick to it."

They unconsciously took each other's hand and walked very slowly through it. It was very difficult not to follow what their brains were telling them about the real world. Marie decided to close her eyes and just to follow Charles. If with her eyes open vertigo was continuously a threat at each pace, with the eyes closed it was more about gravity's pull. Her feet felt like she was walking down a slope but her inner ear was telling her she was going up, and vice versa. It was a terrible experience and one she was never going to get used to. Luckily, Charles was able to guide them through that ordeal. Or was he? She opened her eyes for less than few seconds to find herself in the middle of a huge opening in the corridor. It felt like the corridor was going straight in front and back of her, but not in the exact point she was standing now. It was like walls were bulging out, away from her. She had seen that effect before, a photographer friend of Pierre's who had helped them with the first radiographs. He was using a fish-eye lens for fun and that was exactly what she was seeing in that corridor.

She decided to close her eyes again and follow Charles's lead. They continued to walk for minutes even though her body was telling her that the corridor was barely ten metres long, until they reached a door and she was forced to look again.

31

"That's the canteen. I'm worried to even think about what can happen in there when geometry doesn't follow Euclid," Marie said.

"Well, we need to find that out," Charles said, opening the door.

\*\*\*

Marie had been in this type of canteen before. After her lectures as a student in Warsaw she always went to sit down with her professors if she could. It was the best place and moment to ask more questions without other students around. Other students would look at her with disgust, like she was trying to get favours from the professors. By sitting with the professors she was trespassing over an invisible line – a wall probably would be a better analogy – beyond which she shouldn't have trespassed. It was a tribal-primordial way of thinking, a 'we' against 'them' liturgy as old as the world itself. Her questions, the other students thought, were not asked out of curiosity but only for another aim. *Her scientific interest isn't genuine, she is doing it to show off. She must sit with all of us!*

Marie didn't care about those stares or about the rumours put around by envious girls about her alleged mischievous relationship with a male professor. Someone even told her that rumours had spread about her alleged relationship with a young female professor. It wasn't true, of course – although she had to admit to herself that she did fancy that young woman – and she continued doing it on a daily basis. The professors were very happy with the casual chat about physics and chemistry, and soon they realised that Marie was a precocious young girl who one day, who knows, might get a prestigious place among the gods and goddesses of the scientific pantheon.

"I feel like you are destined to great things," the professor of chemistry told her once while there was no one listening.

On the other hand, they were completely oblivious to what was happening in the background. Marie was hated by almost all the female students, and shunted by everyone else. One evening, when all the students were going back

32

to their quarters to sleep, she was left alone in her room. Her roommate never showed up that night, not even at her hospital bed the day after. Later that night she realised that she had betrayed her by giving the room key to the other girls. They arrived at around midnight, still dressed as if it was day – a sign that they had planned this hours before. She heard the key in the lock, thinking it was her roommate back from a quick adventure in the boys' dormitory, as she sometimes did. The soap bars inside socks, such an old and classic way of getting the shit out of you without the need of a bat, knife or gun. They hit her continuously for minutes until her screams faded to an almost inaudible whisper.

*Is she dead?* she could hear them asking one another. *Maybe it was too much.*

When she woke up at four in the morning she found herself walking barefoot in the canteen, where everything started.

*Did I sleepwalk here, or was I brought here while unconscious?*

She never knew what had happened that night. She had a vague idea of who the perpetrators were, but it was useless to know that as justice would never help her. No proof of who did it. And most of the girls there, unlike her, were daughters of rich and powerful doctors, lawyers and bannisters. She had no chance against them. She was found that morning under a table, shivering like an autumnal leaf, by a janitor.

Her parents came to visit her in the hospital, the only ones who really cared about her. Her father was fuming and she saw him crying outside of her room, hiding his tears from her mum and her. Her mum tried to caress her just where the huge blue and violet bruises were. As her hands were delicately touching her bruised skin she cringed from the excruciating pain. Marie had never suffered so much pain in her life. The doctors said she had been lucky to get out with minor injuries, as it could have been worse. A couple of hits on her head and she could have been in a coffin. One on her rib had possibly caused a fracture, but there was no way of knowing that. How ironic, for she was going to be the inventor of radiography in few years' time!

33

When she approached the canteen door she felt a mixture of emotions. Good times, when she had learned so much and was given equal respect by the professors. And bad times, of course. Months and months of hate around those tables and chairs had culminated in that cowardly attack. And there was some additional irony in that, as that night she ended up scarred and half-naked in the very place where it all started. She tried to concentrate on the good times and she imagined that place during the day, full of people. Long tables from one end to the other, never-ending lines to get food from the kitchens. Loud sounds of cutlery, dishes, laughter and steam on the windowpanes. And that was what she had in her mind when Charles opened the door. But instead of long tables, she saw long strips of wood intertwined and twisted in a precise but still chaotic way. These strips were like ribbons departing from the floor and (never)ending in the middle of the air. They ceased to be tables and they became something else, but cutlery and plates were still on their surfaces, sometimes obeying gravity, other times defying it. Chairs were following the shape of the strips and so were floating in the air.

"Moebius strips," Erwin said.

"What?" asked Marie.

"Moebius strips are surfaces with only one side. You can walk on them and you will be sure to cover all their surface. It's like when you staple a ribbon to form a band, but before you do it you apply a half-twist. It is still Euclidean geometry, though."

"This is Escher's work," Charles said.

"It clearly is. Riemann can deform matter, but this is the work of someone who makes art with matter."

"Yes," whispered Marie, pointing at a dark figure on the far side of the canteen.

And Escher was there, they could see him in the kitchen, his shoulders and head bent on a bench where a dish full of food was, eating something. Somehow, he was so focused on what he was doing that he hadn't realised that three people had walked into the canteen. Immediately, the three scientists ducked to the floor hoping the Moebius strips in front of them could cover their presence.

34

They moved slowly around the first strip, being careful not to be touched by the floating chairs around it. They wanted to take him from behind, by surprise. Escher was still bending over his dinner, munching on something like a vulture on a carcass. Erwin waved his hands to his two mates. Marie followed his instructions and moved silently to the left, Charles to the right. Erwin continued to move forward, straight towards Escher's back. He was stepping closer and closer to his victim when Escher suddenly stopped eating. He straightened his spine and pulled his head back like he was stretching. In that exact moment, the giant strips in the canteen started to spin in the air. They rotated like treadmills but following their Moebian course. Chairs followed. Both Marie and Charles were now ducking to the floor, as the strips could hit their heads at any moment. Erwin was in the centre of the room between two big rotating strips, strips that were now like dangerous vortexes that separated him from his companions.

Escher spun very slowly and he wasn't surprised to see them. It was a trap all along, Erwin realised.

He cleaned his mouth with his sleeve, of what appeared to be ice cream. His face was deformed. His left cheek curved inward, while the right one was protruding more than normal; one eye was looking up, the other down; his jaw was split and diverging like two parallel lines tainted by non-Euclidean geometry. Clearly, moving through non-Euclidean space had certain effects on him.

He lifted his arms and the Moebius strips moved faster and faster. The plates and the cutlery that were on their surface started to detach and flew across the canteen. Some landed on the floor next to Erwin, breaking into a thousand pieces, others hit the walls. Then a plate smashed on Erwin's head, making him almost faint. He fell to the floor and hit his forehead badly. He was so confused that he didn't realise that it was now the turn of the cutlery. A couple of knives ended up in his right calf. He felt the pain much later, when he saw them. It was a rain of plates, pans, glasses, spoons and forks, and soon he was covered. And then, when he had almost given up on his life, he thought of Charles and Marie. He had lost sight of them. Did Escher realise they were three? That thought kept him aloft. The

35

last thing he saw before another plate smashed over his head was Escher's deformed face laughing while, like an orchestra's director, he made everything he could rain down on him.

## Chapter 4
## Entering Escher's Realm

When Charles walked back into the corridor to ask the army if they could borrow a longer and stronger cable as he'd suggested earlier, Marie and Erwin stayed behind what remained of the barricade. They spoke in low voices.

"I trust Charles but I don't trust Escher," Erwin said, pointing at the portal on the wall.

"Could be a trap then? Is this what you are suggesting? Like in the canteen?" Marie said.

Erwin nodded.

"Escher is a trickster, we know that. He loves to play with his victims. It's very likely he wants to invite us into his realm. I still think we should let the army do the job."

"Erwin, you saw what happened to the army. All those poor soldiers, I can't even imagine what happened to their bodies."

"What about our bodies? Why are we going to be different?"

"We *are* different. You saw how Charles managed to restrain Riemann with his eel-snake beast before, if only for a little while, right? And you know what my hands are capable of even though I want to use them as little as possible. Somehow Riemann's powers are unable to fight ours."

"I'm still not convinced, Marie. I wish there was another way."

"But there isn't. This is the first time one of Escher's portals stayed open. And God knows how long it will stay like this."

They saw Charles's beard swinging left and right like a pendulum in the corridor. He was running towards them and waving his hands. At first, they didn't understand what he meant, but then they realised he was asking them to take cover. They ducked behind the barricade with their hands over their heads, not knowing what to expect. Then there was a loud bang and dust everywhere. Charles was next to them when they stood up, looking at the cannon of a tank inside the corridor. The tank reversed out of the corridor in less than a minute, leaving behind only rubble.

"It was the only way to get a jeep in with a cable reel."

A pair of soldiers stepped in through the hole the tank had made in the wall, rifles pointing at Escher's portal. The look in their faces was telling. They didn't want to meet the same fate as their mates. One of them waved to someone outside and a jeep drove in, somehow managing to climb on top of the rubble. They fled immediately after, leaving the jeep on top of the rubble just behind the barricade.

"They gave us this jeep with a fifty-metre cable attached to a winch. We've got fifty metres of additional cable that we can join together to make a hundred-metre safety line. The winch is strong enough to move a ten-ton lorry. We don't have much time. They will intervene if we don't get out in an hour."

"Good job, Charles," Erwin said, patting his shoulder.

"Let's get it working then," Marie said, reaching out to the winch.

They secured the cable to Charles's waist with a snap hook and released the security block to get the cable loose.

"I'm coming with you, but I still think this will be a trap," Erwin said, grabbing his wooden box.

Charles looked at him for a moment and then said: "Erwin, you are free to stay here if you want to."

"No, I'll be helping you. I have nothing to lose, and by the way, the world as we know it will probably be destroyed, so does it matter?" he said with a smile.

"Let's hope we can avoid it though," Charles said with a grin.

38

They moved closer to the portal. Rising flights of steps, upside-down towers, doors opening to nowhere and anywhere: it was truly the representation of madness. If geometry can be evil, this was it.

A far away howling brought their minds back to the monster they had created.

"What do we do with Newton? It was going to be our weapon, right?" asked Erwin, looking at Charles.

"It had superpowers even before we gave them to it." Charles touched his nose with his index finger. "I'm sure it can find its way to us by using its sense of smell."

"Times three," Marie added.

"And talking about smell..." Charles took a piece of cloth that was hanging from the radiator and put it in his pocket.

Erwin, despite his doubts, was the first to step into the portal. He moved his foot forward, crossing the boundary between the two worlds. He waited to see if anything would happen to it but it looked normal, although he could see a change in its colour. Escher's world was black and white, and his foot moved from colour to grey then to black and white. It was like becoming part of the drawing.

Marie was going to do the same when she stopped abruptly.

"Did I just hear a meow coming out of your wooden box?"

Erwin spun around and smiled at her.

"Are you kidding me? You've got a live cat in there? All this time? And what about that smell?"

Now Erwin pushed further in and slowly slid his whole body through, leaving her behind. Marie looked at Charles in disbelief.

"Hardly surprising," Charles said, looking at her. "Everyone knows that Erwin Schrodinger loves cats."

***

Charles followed Erwin and invited Marie to follow him, taking her hand. She let it go and, closing her eyes, she walked through. It felt for a little while like their bodies touched the surface of a pond, but they were still dry.

39

They entered Escher's realm and immediately became part of it. They became black and white, and it seemed like their figures were drawn with a pencil.

If it wasn't for Erwin standing in front of them with his little wooden box on his back, it would have felt like it was a dream. His body was giving them some idea of the proportions inside that world.

It was as if they had infinite possibilities of movement in all directions. Flight of stairs leading nowhere and everywhere. The ceiling – if you could call it that – was covered in steps and doors and mezzanines and hanging passages. It was an architectural jungle and the canopy was made of stairs.

They looked at each other and smiled at their new silhouettes.

"It's like being in a comic," Erwin said, looking at his black and white hands.

Marie looked back at the corridor they'd left behind in the real world. She could see the jeep on top of the rubble, the cable coming out of the winch and finishing at Charles's waist. It was the only object in between the two worlds.

While they were mesmerised by the new world's aesthetics, Charles started to call for Newton, shouting as loud as he could.

"What if Escher can hear us?" Marie said, holding his arm tightly.

"I suspect he already knows we are here, so it doesn't make that much difference."

As he finished saying that they heard Newton, like a pack of stray dogs going crazy at the sight of a cat. The barking was coming from above them, exactly on top of their heads. They saw it upside-down, looking at them, twisting its heads like when dogs can't understand a command from a human. Even Newton couldn't cope with this crazy environment. Charles was calling it and telling it to come their way. Newton stepped down from the stairs and went in through a door. He disappeared and reappeared on their left on another flight of stairs that was going up sideways. There was no way he could find his way to them.

"It's impossible, Charles," Marie said.

40

"We need him so he can take us to Riemann," Charles said, waving the piece of cloth that he had taken from the radiator.

Charles continued to call the Cerberus for minutes but each door or stair that it headed to it wasn't only in the wrong direction, but also on the wrong side. The dog's heads continued to twist to the side in disbelief: those humans were down, and now were they were on one side.

While this was happening, Marie grabbed Erwin's arm and forced him to turn towards them.

"I think we deserve some sort of an explanation about that," she said, pointing at the box.

"I don't think it's the right time for this, Marie," Charles said.

"It's okay, Charles, I owe you this," Erwin said, placing the wooden box on the floor.

He knelt on the floor and started to loosen the ropes.

"As you know, the day of the Gottingen Accident I wasn't there with you, but my office, a few corridors along from the accident room, was struck by the blast. Charles was right when he said that I love cats. Actually, I had four of them in the office at the time. Only one survived the blast that day though. I found the other three lying on the floor, disturbingly deformed. I found them like they were begging for mercy, they must have been suffering unimaginable pain, like the human victims of that day."

"But one survived," repeated Marie, looking at the box.

"One survived, if you can say that."

He opened the lid of the box and a terrible smell of rotten meat came out of it. They all had to cover their faces in repulsion. The creature that jumped out of it was bizarre to say the least, and any human language would have been challenged to find the right words to describe it. It was a cat, that was obvious, that was simultaneously alive and dead. Now, how is that possible? Marie couldn't believe her eyes. It was like two images, of a live cat and a dead cat, were juxtaposed, or even better overlaid one on top of the other. There was some transparency playing within it and continuous flickering as well. The live cat could move its body anywhere like a normal cat, but the dead one was still – how surprising! – so that even though the creature as a

41

whole could move from one point to the other, it was only the live cat that was actually walking with its legs. The dead cat was simply appearing and disappearing every now and then and its body was lying at the live cat's paws. The flickering was disturbing to the eyes, like a neon lamp in its final minutes of life, but there was an old projector effects quality to it that made it fascinating too.

"It's a quantum cat. It is both live and dead. It came from a thought experiment I designed to ridicule some of my colleagues who thought that particles could be simultaneously in different states until an observer intervenes. There was a Geiger counter, a radioactive material and… but there is no need to go through all this. What you need to know is that I wrote this down on my blackboard in the office, and somehow the blast passed through my formulas on the wall and transferred it to one of my cats, Tabby."

"Which is now the living dead, a zombie."

"Technically, it's in a superpositional state, both alive and dead. But you can call it a zombie if you like."

"But why did you bring it with you?"

"Well, first of all you can't kill a dead cat, can you?"

"I guess not."

"So, we have an immortal cat at our disposal, and with Charles's help and maybe yours we might be able to come up with something… rather peculiar."

"Yeah, like what happened with Newton," Marie said sarcastically.

"Talking about that," Erwin said, pointing at the closest flight of stairs to them.

The creature was descending the stairs at speed, all three heads pointing at them, like a hound hunting for a hare in the woods. Howling like a hunter.

It was scary. And unstoppable. Charles tried to put himself between it and Marie and Erwin, but the beast simply jumped too high over his head. Only one of its paws slapped Charles's face and pushed him to the floor. But when it landed it was immediately clear that its target wasn't Erwin or Marie. It was the cat.

What followed was a gruesome scene. Newton's central head grabbed the cat's body in the air while it was

42

jumping away. The left head didn't waste time and stabbed its thighs with its fangs. They both pulled in opposite directions and the cat was screaming with pain... intermittently. Every now and then the cat was dead and didn't emit any sound or move. Its flesh was ripping apart very easily in its dead version, spraying dark and dense blood mixed with pus. By the time the right head started to grab the cat's head, the other two heads stopped, clearly disgusted by the taste of the carcass. After a while, Newton released its grip on the cat altogether.

Although the live cat shouldn't have survived such an attack, it clearly did. It was meowing like nothing had happened to it and started to lick its intimate parts in front of everyone like any normal cat would do; apart from when it was dead, obviously.

"I told you, you can't kill it," Erwin said, stroking its head, being careful to stop when the dead version appeared.

Marie was visibly shocked and didn't say a word for a few minutes. Charles managed to calm Newton down and started to use the piece of cloth.

"Well, at least we got Newton back, we proved that he is a formidable hunter and that Erwin's cat is immortal," Charles said with a smile.

"Now Newton, find Riemann. Find him!" said Charles, waving the piece of cloth in front of the three heads.

Newton started to sniff the ground and the three heads decided simultaneously where to go.

"I have to say, I didn't expect that," Erwin said while he put Tabby back in the box. "I expected the three heads to have different opinions on the track, but it seems like they are working together pretty efficiently."

Once finished with the box he gave his hand to Marie, who was sitting on the floor still shocked from what had happened.

"Better now?"

She nodded and she let him pull her up.

"Let's follow Charles and Newton then, before we lose them!"

They ran behind Charles, who in turn was running behind Newton up the stairs. The cable was always in the way and there were times when they tripped on it. Up the stairs, then they turned left but this was upside-down, then they turned right where a door let them into a mezzanine that was facing diagonally on their left. They went down the next flight of stairs, but it was like going up. After a sharp left turn, Marie saw Newton and Charles appear next to her upside-down, but they were in front of her a second ago. When she turned left herself, she caught a glimpse of Erwin's leg next to her where she was coming from, but Erwin's body was behind her. How could he be in two places at the same time? Then she just forced herself to look straight ahead and not ask questions. The secret was not to look around you, just ahead of you.

Newton seemed unaffected by the lack of logic now, and was focusing almost entirely on the smell. He stopped at a locked door and started to scratch at the wood. Of all the doors they passed by, it had stopped at this one only. For a reason: Riemann was likely behind it.

"This is it. This is the exit from the labyrinth," Charles said, reaching for the handle.

"Wait," Marie said, stopping his hand. "Let me see what's behind it first."

She placed her hands on the wood and closed her eyes. They started to become hot red, and when the colour changed to white magma figures started to appear on the wood like radiographs. They were like ghosts, skeletons of objects from the other side. There was a sofa with the frame well defined but with the rest somewhat recognisable; two chairs, a table, a vase with a plant, a small cabinet with what appeared to be books. It was an apartment and there was no one in it. Although something was wrong.

"It seems safe and empty of people but it's all..." she said slowly and taking deep breaths, for she was exhausted by the use of her powers.

The handle gave easily, no locking system. Charles was the first to get in and... he jumped up, disappearing. The cable followed his body up too. Marie and Erwin didn't move a single muscle. In a way, they expected everything but that. Charles went up and disappeared. They heard him shouting and swearing from the ceiling of the apartment.

Erwin pushed his head in, being careful not to step in. He saw Charles lying on the ceiling next to the lamp.

"Are you okay?"

"Kind of. Hopefully I have no broken bones. What happened?"

"You went up."

"Yeah, I figured that out myself, thanks."

Erwin took a coin from his pocket and threw it into the room, and the coin fell up to the ceiling.

"Gravity. It's upside-down in this room."

"We can pull you up using the cable, which is very handy."

"Why don't you come down, I mean up? This is definitely the right place. Newton smelled it up until here."

He stood up and his head was almost touching the surface of the table. It took them a while to realise that Charles's colours were back to normal.

"There! Another door." He pointed to his left, where a big green door stood.

"What does he say?" asked Marie.

"He asked us to follow him down, well up there really. There is another door, apparently."

They descended one by one, making sure the reversal of gravity was not going to let them crash into the ceiling as had happened with Charles. They hung from the door and jumped up. Newton simply jumped and fell onto his back without any trouble or surprise. It was becoming accustomed to unexpected physics. Their comic-like black and white silhouette was gone. Now that they were all walking on the ceiling with their heads upside-down, they moved to the next door. Marie repeated her magic again but this time she felt exhausted, her face pale like the moon.

"Every time I use it I feel so weak."

"It sucks up a lot of your energy, Marie," Charles said, giving her his hand to stand up.

"Did you see what's behind the door?"

"Just a glimpse of a corridor and more furniture. It's like the rest of a house."

"Well, let's hope gravity is not playing tricks again," Erwin said, asking Charles to help him reach the handle, which was now too high to reach.

The door opened into a corridor with more doors and a flight of stairs to their right. There were a lot of framed drawings on the walls. It was all Escher's work: one of them looked exactly like the strange world they had passed through minutes earlier. Another was like a puzzle made of flying geese, whose negative silhouettes made up other geese flying in the opposite direction. Another one with flying geese that transformed into fish below the surface of the water. A hand holding a glass globe with Escher's reflection on it. Then a photo of Escher with a woman, his wife presumably.

"It's Escher's house," whispered Erwin, throwing another coin into the corridor. Gravity was the same as in the room where they were now.

They moved into the corridor by climbing on the wall (luckily it was an old house with low ceilings) and Charles said something from the back of the queue.

"Cable is over, guys."

The cable had finished its length and was stretching in the air from his waist.

"I have to tie it here. And we have to go ahead without it. At least we passed through the labyrinth and this will be our chance to get out."

He tied it to a leg of the table.

Erwin signed silence with his index finger on his lips. They didn't know if the house was inhabited now.

They had to proceed along the ceiling of the corridor until they reached the stairs. Newton was pointing at the floor but was still stuck on the ceiling. He was unable to track the smell of Riemann from there.

"I guess Newton won't be of any help from now on and we will need to find Riemann ourselves," Charles whispered, pointing at the confused dog.

They walked along the ceiling of the corridor until it reached the stairs. They simply walked up onto the ceiling of the stairs, which in their case was a smooth ramp. The ground floor was comprised of a lounge, kitchen and an entrance hall. The door was art deco and through its glass they could see the road. A busy road. But it seemed like everyone and the cars were walking in the right gravitational pull.

46

"Are you thinking the same as I'm thinking?" whispered Charles to Erwin. "Reverse gravity affects only us but not the furniture in the house, or the people outside of the house."

"Is it us who are wrong, then?"

"I don't know, it might be a discrimination between inanimate objects and living beings."

"What about that then?"

Marie pointed at a small finch in a cage in the lounge. The bird was sitting on its perch just fine and hadn't seen them yet. Erwin and Charles looked each other in the eyes.

"It's us."

"Perhaps passing through that labyrinth affected our... physics?" Erwin suggested.

"How do we go back to normal gravity?"

"Don't know. It's Escher's world, we need to play by its rules."

"It's seems that he isn't in the house, by the way. Otherwise he would have heard you guys talking by now," Marie said in a sarcastic tone.

Erwin decided to ignore her comment, and said in a loud voice: "Well, if he is not in, would you excuse me?" and he went straight to the fridge.

"I'm starving. We haven't eaten since this morning."

He reached for the top of the fridge but it was too high for him to reach anything inside. Charles went to his aid and placed his hands in a cup gesture. Erwin stepped on his hands and hung onto the fridge, taking a carton of milk, some cake and eggs. They all started to eat the cake and they passed the milk around. The eggs went in Newton's mouths.

Since that morning when they'd been summoned by the police to help against Riemann they hadn't eaten, let alone rested or stopped. They realised how exhausted they were only now, standing on the ceiling of Escher's house. A ceiling where there were no chairs, sofas or beds, obviously. They simply sat on the ceiling, now completely used to the weirdness of the situation. After so much stress and tension this was the first time they could relax. They felt cheerful, almost giddy.

47

"It's like being like a gecko," Erwin said. "Geckos with their incredible feet have superpowers, like you lot."

"Like walking on ceilings but being unable to reach bread in the kitchen?" Marie said, pointing at a loaf of bread too high to be within their reach.

"Well, a gecko can actually reach objects by throwing its tongue."

"That's a chameleon," Marie said.

"Maybe I can make them evolve on you, Erwin. A chameleon's tongue and a gecko's feet," Charles said, visibly exhausted.

Erwin looked at the old man who was lying next to the lamp for few seconds, hoping he was kidding.

"Charles, have you ever experimented with your powers on humans by any chance?"

The answer arrived after a while.

"No, and I don't think it's ethically acceptable."

"What if the person asks you to do it?"

"Still I think it would be wrong."

"Why?"

"I still don't know what the side effects are."

"What d'you mean?"

Charles helped himself up, so he could sit.

"Some of my finches died after a few days. Others developed... things I don't want to describe right now, especially after eating that delicious cake."

"All?"

"No, some survived and are still alive to this day. It's gambling with mutations, Erwin. One day you've got Icarus wings, the day after you are a blob of flesh and pus. That's it."

"Luckily you said you didn't want to describe it, eh?" said a disgusted Marie.

"Why? Why are you asking, Erwin?" Charles said with a grin on his face.

"Just curious."

Marie looked at him sideways. "Come on."

"Well, if you insist. You all have powers, even my cat has powers for God's sake. I'm the only one here without any. Is it that far-fetched, to wish for some?"

"Our lives are not that 'bowl of cherries' that you think," said a distant Marie.

Erwin sighed. "Look, I know the pain that it gave you, but I just want to help."

"But you are. You saved my life, don't you remember?" said Charles, eating the last bit of cake

Yes, he was right. There in the canteen that morning, Erwin had saved his life against the wrath of Escher. The last thing Erwin remembered after being completely covered with hundreds of plate fragments and cutlery was the grin on Escher's deformed face. Then he passed out for what he thought were seconds, but were actually minutes. Escher was beating Charles, who was no match for him. Marie was on the floor unconscious. Either Escher had beat her or a flying plate hit her. Erwin wasn't sure what had happened while he was passed out. He pulled himself together and stood up on top of the porcelain fragments. It was then that he realised a knife was still inside his calf. He pulled it out and a stream of blood came out. It was painful but the situation was desperate. So, he advanced towards Escher, limping and in pain, until he managed to plant the knife in Escher's shoulder. Escher screamed with pain and let Charles go. His face changed conformation and where there was a bump, now it was a hole, and vice versa. His skin and flesh were like boiling magma and were continuously changing the shape of his face.

Escher tried to pull the knife out of his shoulder but couldn't. The pain was excruciating. And that was affecting his creations as well. The Moebius table strips stopped spinning around. It was the right moment to escape, Erwin thought. He reached for Charles and shouted at him to stand up. Together they grabbed Marie's arms and dragged her along the floor to the main door. Escher didn't realise or he was in too much pain to care, but he eventually managed to get the knife out. With a scream of pain, his everchanging face like a cuttlefish skin, he started to walk towards them. And in doing so the strips started to spin again in the air. This time he was moving them like gigantic chainsaws, ready to dismember their bodies alive.

"Charles, move on! Quick, quick!"

49

It wasn't easy. Charles was badly hit and punched by Escher. He was covered in bruises and his age wasn't helping. Erwin was limping and bleeding. Marie was still unconscious and it wasn't clear what had happened to her. Later, Charles told Erwin that Marie saw Erwin fall under the plate fragments and jumped on Escher's back, taking him by surprise. She had put her hands over his face, hoping she could fry his brain with X-rays, but Escher simply threw her to the floor and kicked her head repeatedly. It was then that Charles moved in to help her but he was badly beaten.

They reached the far end of the room and found the door locked. The only other way of escape was the door they came in through on their left. But between the door and them there was Escher and his moving weapons. They were trapped, and it was clear that this was the end of their adventure. Riemann and his clique of geometry-perverters had won.

Escher was advancing slowly now because he knew it was a matter of minutes to his victory. The Moebius strips were advancing at the same pace, making Erwin's and Charles's last minutes even more dreadful. But life is full of surprises, and while everyone in the room had either given up or was joyfully thinking of a victory, Marie did not. She woke up and without standing she started to emit X-rays from her hands towards the lock of the door. She used an awful amount of her energy to fuse the inner mechanisms of the lock, but it worked. When she stood up shouting, "All of you, get out!" Erwin and Charles couldn't believe their eyes. The door opened with a simple kick and quickly they were out. Escher realised too late and he ran quickly behind them, followed by the strips. They smashed into the wall, too big to get through the door and too weak to cut through the wall. When Escher reached the door they were gone, through another door and into another long corridor.

## Chapter 5
## The Hatch

They heard the lock of the door clicking. Two men were chatting casually outside. They could see their figures through the art deco glass of the door. Erwin and Charles quickly stood up and grabbed Newton's fur.

"Quick, upstairs!" said Erwin, pulling both Charles and the beast up. Marie was dozing off against the wall and was caught in the commotion. They managed to reach the first floor walking on the ceiling, just before a dark figure came into the house. Erwin pointed at the loft hatch without saying anything. They opened it and descended into the loft, pulling Newton in. Strangely, the dog didn't bark and was relatively quiet, and that simplified the operation. Erwin lowered the hatch but Marie stopped him.

"You are not coming with us?" she whispered, almost hissing.

"The hatch can only be opened from outside. You need me here so I can get you out. Remember, I don't have powers but I can still help." He finished the last word with a smile.

The hatch closed with a soft click and he crawled across the ceiling. He could hear two men chatting below in the lounge. One was Escher, the other he had no clue. He focused his attention on the conversation as much as he could.

"Would you like a bit of whisky?"

"Yes, a glass would help."

51

Sounds of liquid and glasses on a table. Someone sat down on the sofa.

"Ahh."

"Still pain?"

"Yes, that Austrian bastard pushed the knife to the bone. Hope he didn't touch a nerve."

"You would have known by now."

Erwin couldn't help smiling.

The second man sat on a chair not far from Escher. Clearly, they were not affected by reverse gravity as they themselves had been. Maybe it was because they were not tainted by non-Euclidean geometry, or because something happened to them when they passed through Escher's realm. That got Erwin thinking in the back of his mind while he was listening to the small talk between the two.

"So, what did you want to talk about, Carl?" asked Escher.

*Gauss!*

Carl Gauss waited a few seconds before answering, as he was sipping his whisky.

"Riemann."

"What about him?"

"I'm worried."

"You shouldn't be. He knows what he is doing."

"I know him well, Maurits. I was his mentor for many years. But I've never seen him so…"

"So wild?" asked Escher with a laugh.

"Yeah, since he wrote that non-Euclidean formula on his forehead with a knife – which I think is by itself very gory, and a sign of some mental disturbance – he lost his mind."

"Well, don't run too fast now. That was necessary for him to get full control over reality. I supervised that moment."

"A bloody ritual like a tribal initiation."

"I concede the method was a bit… unorthodox, but it was essential for our plans. Do I have to remind you that before that he had to write formulas on the objects to modify reality? How do you think he would have been able to stop the army or those scientists that they now think are superheroes?"

52

"I know, I know, but his head loses control from time to time, you know?"

"And that's why he is working on a solution."

"Solution? What solution?"

"He found out that using a special helmet made of non-Euclidean metal – don't ask what the hell that is! – helps in blocking his bursts of energy."

"Does it work?"

"It really works. Up to a certain level. I've seen it in action and it can block the minor bursts but not the major ones. But he is working on a better version right now."

"I didn't know about this. It's reassuring but I still think we should have a different approach to the plan."

"What do you mean?"

"Maurits, you know that my initial approach was different. It was good when we were going around universities explaining about the advantages of non-Euclidean geometry over Euclidean. It was the right way. Not by killing innocent soldiers and who knows how many fellow scientists!"

"Carl, you need to put everything into context. That mob of scientists was attacking us."

"They were protesting!"

"No, you know about the mob's dynamics. We could have been lynched that day. Riemann saved us!"

"Saved us by killing God knows how many of them."

"I hope you are not going to argue about self-defence. And by the way, some of them survived and got... gifts. They should thank us."

"Yes, that they are going to use against us. Look, I still believe in our project. It's just that I think we should take the reins now. Riemann's job is done, now it's time for us to put some reason into this."

"You are talking about mutiny. I'm going to pretend I didn't hear you, Carl."

"But listen, Maurits. It is not mutiny when the captain has lost his reason and is directing the ship towards the rocks. He will destroy the world and us with it."

There was silence for more than a minute. Someone drank from a glass and then left it on the coffee table. Possibly Escher.

"Let's see how the situation develops in the next few hours and then we will talk about it again," Escher said very hieratically. "That ultimate weapon in Gottingen that Riemann is talking about all the time still needs to be built. Maybe we can instil some reason before he finishes it."

"Deal," Gauss said.

They stood up and walked to the door.

"Before I go," Gauss said. "Talking about Curie, Darwin and Schrodinger – I know that you hate them, and for good reason."

Erwin imagined Gauss pointing at Escher's shoulder and the latter frowning at the pain.

"Sometimes it is better to get the powerful on your side rather than opposing them. What I'm trying to say is that we might be able to talk to them and explain why we are doing what we are doing. With their powers on our side we will be invincible."

"We are already invincible, Carl. It's just a matter of time before I kill them all. And you will forget about them, let me assure you."

"Fine. I'll see you tonight in my office for the official meeting with Riemann. He should arrive at nine."

The door opened, and after a couple of goodbyes it closed again. And there was silence. Only Escher's steps on the wooden floor and... barking. Coming from the loft. Loud barking. Howling too, coming from three dogs.

"Shit," hissed Erwin, going back to the loft hatch.

He heard Escher climbing up the stairs. Erwin managed to flatten himself on a dark part of the ceiling, so Escher did not see him. Escher understood where the barking was coming from but he wasn't taking any action. The last thing he expected was to hear a dog barking in his loft! He ran down as fast as he could and came back with a double-barrelled shotgun. He loaded it and waited for the next bark. He shot at the hatch and again at the ceiling where he thought the sound was coming from. Erwin didn't have the courage to intervene. His enemy was holding a shotgun and was standing on the "right" gravity side of the corridor. The barking resumed and for a moment it seemed like Newton was scratching at the hatch.

*They can't open it from the inside!* thought Erwin.

54

"Whoever is there, come out, or I swear I'll fill your guts with hot lead!" Escher shouted while reloading the shotgun.

The sound of multiple steps in the loft, actually on the roof, was a sign for Escher that there was more than one, apart from the dogs of course. He stepped back, thinking about this new revelation.

"What the hell..."

He shot again at different points on the ceiling.

"Stop it! Stop it!" a feminine voice came from inside the loft.

"Who the hell are you? Come down slowly or I'll shoot again."

"Impossible," was the reply.

"What?"

"The hatch. It can only be opened from the outside."

Escher didn't say anything, but it was clear that he was growing more and more suspicious. He didn't want to get too close to the hatch, thinking it was a trap. And knowing Marie and Charles, Erwin thought he was right to be prudent. He waited, keep pointing the tip of the shotgun at the hatch. Erwin thought about taking the chance now, but he wasn't an action man and after what had happened in the canteen that morning he was still fearful of Escher. There was a bestial side to him that made him shiver.

Escher stepped back and almost stopped just below Erwin's head. Erwin flattened himself as close as possible to the ceiling, hoping Escher didn't realise he had a man attached to the ceiling above his head. Then Escher's face rotated to the side, almost like he was following the track of a smell. He sniffed the air several times and his face shifted to disgusted.

*The cat!* Erwin thought, and his heart skipped a beat.

His nose had become accustomed to the rotten smell by now, but for Escher it was surely the most disgusting smell he had ever smelled. Luckily, the ceiling was the last place where someone would check for rotten remains. So, Escher started to poke his nose into a cabinet, even on a desk and in a vase and the bathroom, always with the gun pointed towards the hatch. He couldn't find the source of the smell and he was growing restless.

55

"Who are you?" he shouted at the hatch. "And why did you take a corpse into the loft?"

It took a few moments for Charles to reply.

"Escher, you know very well who we are and why we are here. Regarding the corpse: that's Erwin's cat and it's dead and we can't do anything about it, I'm afraid."

"Darwin, Curie and Schrodinger. You bastards, you will die now," Escher said shooting at the hatch again.

Newton must have been hit by a bullet because it suddenly yelped, followed by whining from all three heads.

"What the fuck? You've got dead cats and a pack of dogs up there?"

The moment he said that, a sudden crash came from one of the rooms. It was the same room they had first came in from. This was followed by the voices of several men. Escher jumped with surprise. He opened the door with a kick and saw the half-smashed table pulled up to the portal. A metal cable was tied to its leg, and it was clear someone from the other side of the portal had pulled it so that the table had crashed into the portal, but it was too big to get through it.

"Shit. I forgot to close the portal," Escher said, lowering the gun and moving closer to the table to inspect it.

Voices were coming from the other side of the portal, but it wasn't clear who they were and what they were saying.

It was the right moment for Erwin. He couldn't hope for a better opportunity to open the hatch. He quickly crawled to the hatch and opened it, and whispered: "It's me. Come out immediately now!"

First to come out was Marie, then Charles. Newton was wounded in his hind leg. Charles and Erwin had to lift him up through the hatch.

Escher didn't realise what had happened. He almost forgot about the hatch, probably thinking that they couldn't get out from there anyway. All three moved closer to the open door, hoping they could quickly make a plan to attack Escher from the back without being harmed, but they stood at the threshold as a bizarre scene unfolded in front of them.

56

A stronger pull of the cable broke the table completely and pulled the remaining pieces inside the portal, leaving the portal fully open. Several dark shapes were running up and down and left and right on the stairs. It became clear after a while that they were soldiers following the cable to the portal. The cable was zigzagging all over, which was why the soldiers looked so scattered in the crazy landscape.

Escher immediately realised he was in danger. He grabbed the table leg that was still attached to the cable and threw it into the portal. The winch now was pulling the cable away through the stairs, but five or six soldiers were close enough that they didn't need to follow the cable anymore. They could see the portal and they could see Escher peeking through a door. A door that represented an escape route away from that crazy world. Escher quickly put one of his hands on the portion of the wall that was framing the portal. Slowly, second by second, the portal started to shrink. One of the soldiers shouted something to the others behind him and started to run faster, almost in desperation. Escher loved that and started to laugh while the portal was shrinking little by little. He was enjoying their panic. He wanted to lock them inside his world. Buried alive, doomed to wander around the creation of a madman forever.

Marie, Charles and Erwin could see this scene clearly from the corridor, behind Escher's back. They were hoping the soldiers would arrive as quickly as possible at the portal. But it was clear they wouldn't make it. Even the soldier who had shouted aloud, now on his knees, desperately trying to point his rifle to Escher's direction. He shot a couple of times, but Escher ducked behind the wall. He didn't need to be in front of the portal to close it.

Erwin moved forward and Charles understood he wanted to stop Escher. He grasped his arm and pulled him back. It was too dangerous, with bullets flying astray from the portal and Escher still with his shotgun in his hand. A shotgun that he was now pointing inside the portal. He wanted to hit that soldier. He shot once, aiming without any real effort, and missed. As soon as it was shot though, Newton jumped forward and ran along the ceiling like a train, bypassing Marie, Charles and Erwin. For the first time Escher looked back to the corridor, alarmed by Newton's

57

growling. His face was so shocked by what he saw that his deformed jaw dropped and split even further in two where the chin was. He probably had a few milliseconds to realise that his life was over, that he had underestimated those three scientists, that he had forgotten about the hatch and many other mistakes that surely came to his mind just before Newton's central head clasped his own head from above and dragged him inside the portal. Newton landed inside the other world and immediately rolled down a staircase with its victim still clutched to it. Escher was barely visible now. One arm here and one leg there, sticking out from underneath the dog's body and the fury of the heads in that attacking frenzy.

Two soldiers were now so close to the scene that they had to step away to avoid being tangled up in the fight. Less than a fight now that Escher's body seemed shredded to bits, though. Newton knew its victim was over but continued to mutilate him. Guess that was revenge for the bullet in his thigh.

With Escher dead, his power grab on reality vanished all of a sudden. Gravity reversed and they fell to the floor.

"My bones," Charles said, standing up slowly.

There was a lot of complaining from the fallen, and it took them a while to realise that the portal was closing. Erwin jumped forward in a desperate attempt to reach the wall but the shrinking portal perimeter completely ignored his hands. He grabbed it for the last few seconds but there was nothing in the world that could stop its closure. The last thing he saw was one of the soldiers' faces from the other side pleading to get him out. He felt Charles's hand on his shoulder.

"It's over, Erwin. The portal is closed forever. Let's hope those poor souls will find a good way to pass away now."

They sat in the room, spread between sofa and chairs. Exhausted, they stayed speechless for several long minutes. Escher was dead, Newton had saved them giving up its life, and all those soldiers were doomed to walk in that perverted space forever. The only way to escape was now closed. Anyone would think their morale was down to the floor now, but they couldn't be more wrong.

"We made it guys," Marie said with a spark of joy on her eyes. "Thanks to Newton the world is safer without Escher."

"Poor Newton. He was a good dog. Now we need to stop Riemann though," Charles said.

"Yes, it's true, but Escher was his right hand and we got rid of him. Gauss is next."

Erwin came back to life and looked at them.

"No need to get rid of Gauss."

Erwin told them about the conversation he had overheard earlier in the lounge. Gauss's doubts about Riemann, his willingness to talk to them and get them on their side, and about the ultimate weapon Riemann was preparing.

"You are suggesting we talk to Gauss to make him see reason?"

"Yes, I'm tired of violence and death. Maybe with him we can work differently. Maybe we can talk to him."

"And how are you planning to find him?"

He pointed at the White Pages book next to the phone in a corner of the room.

"His office. But before nine."

# Chapter 6
## Gauss's Office

It was eight in the evening and they were walking the streets slowly and quietly to keep a low profile. They didn't know those streets and they didn't know who – if anyone – was collaborating with Riemann or Gauss, so it was better not to ask questions. Charles's beard was extremely – and internationally – recognisable, so he tried to hide it as much as he could with his coat but at times he looked decisively awkward. It didn't help that Erwin was still limping from the stabbing in his calf and Marie was pale and weak like a malaria patient. So, despite their efforts they attracted few glances from the passers-by. They ignored them and kept straight on, hoping there were no informants around.

They had no time to make any plan as they wanted to talk to Gauss before nine, before Riemann's arrival. They will have to improvise as they always did in that long day. It had worked out well so far.

Dr Carl Gauss, Winterstraße 78.

They didn't want to appear all three at his door, so Marie volunteered to knock while the other two were waiting in the dark alley at the corner. She tried to stay awake and standing straight so as not to look sick. She inhaled a good breath of autumn air and knocked at the green door in front of her. No answer. She knocked again. Then she suspected Gauss wasn't opening it because he was expecting a door-knock code of some sort. She avoided looking at the corner of the alley a few metres away, so as not to give her friends' cover away.

60

She tried a third time, then she walked away. She met with the others.

"If this is the address, he is either not in or he is not opening because he is expecting a code."

"Damn it!"

"We have to get in before nine. We must talk to him now."

"Any idea?"

"We break in," Erwin said, pointing at a half open window of the two-storey house.

The window was too high to reach. Erwin tried to push Marie up with his hands clamped in a cup shape but it was still too high. Charles ran to the far end of the alley and grabbed a rubbish bin. In dragging it he made quite a lot of noise. A dog started to bark nearby and Charles stopped until it finished. They all thought about Newton, the Cerberus hero that had saved the world. It seemed so far away in time now, but it was just a few hours ago. Erwin went to help and they lifted the bin so it wouldn't make too much noise. This time Marie didn't volunteer, she sat on the ground with her hand on her forehead. She was weaker and weaker the more time was passing. Erwin jumped up onto the bin and after a couple of attempts managed to grab the sill. He lifted himself up in a way that amazed both Marie and Charles.

"I didn't know he was so athletic," mumbled Charles.

Once in, Erwin found an empty room. The wallpaper was ripped and was flopping down to the floor. Some of the wooden boards were missing. Spiderwebs covered most of the corners. Windowpanes were shattered all over the floor. The door was missing, and he later found it down the flight of stairs. The whole place smelled of mothballs. It looked like the house had been left abandoned for decades. Was it the right address? Were they too late now to find the right house? He was going to say it to his friends from the window when he heard a door shutting. It was from downstairs. He walked down the stairs, trying not to make too much noise. Some of the wooden boards were either broken or missing so he needed to be careful. He reached the ground floor but saw all the doors either open or smashed/ripped or lying on the floor. None was shut like

61

he'd imagined from the sound he'd heard. He decided to let the others in by the main door, as the house looked empty. He saw Charles on the other side of the road with his wooden box, probably anticipating that he was going to open the front door soon. Once in, they quickly realised something wasn't as they'd expected.

"Wrong house?" Marie whispered, while she was trying to find a place to sit. Save for a couple of half-broken cabinets, the house was empty of furniture.

Erwin lifted his index finger to his mouth.

"I think we are not alone," he whispered, pointing at the basement hatch in the kitchen.

They opened it slowly and saw a distant light coming from inside. They decided to go in. It was a green glowing light, fading to a barely detectable fluorescence at times. They stepped down the rusty little ladder very slowly, Erwin leading the way. If it wasn't for the fact that they knew they were in a basement of an old house, that place did not look like a basement at all. It was a fully decorated and functional house. *Functional* meaning not only that all the appliances in the kitchen and bathroom and the electricity were working and so on, but even the windows (yes, there were windows in the basement) were "functional". Erwin had to look twice at the hatch through which they had come down to believe his eyes. The window in the small lounge he was looking at was open and there were trees and a busy road brightened by a sizzling summer midday sun. It was as if the house they'd left upstairs, abandoned at night during a slightly chilly autumn day, was just a loft to this underground house.

"An underground world?" Marie whispered to his face.

"More likely that hatch was a portal. We are probably in another place, and who knows where on earth."

"At least we know it's Gauss's office," Charles said, pointing at the official framed degree certificate that was hanging on a wall.

Their first encounter with Carl Gauss was unexpected and incredibly brief. He popped out from one of the doors that were facing the main corridor holding a glass of water. He didn't scream, and neither did they. They all simply looked at each other, puzzled and still. When Gauss realised there were intruders in his office, he dropped the glass and dashed into another room as if he was being chased by a man-eating tiger.

Their reactions were slow and they started chasing him, too late to grab him. They then heard him running down the stairs and they followed. They ran as quickly as they could despite Erwin's limping leg, Marie's weakness and Charles's age. They wanted to finish this once and for all. They rammed through a door until they saw the barrel of the gun.

"I got enough bullets to kill you all in seconds. And shoot your dead bodies again."

"That won't be necessary," Erwin said, stepping back with his hands in the air.

"I bloody hope so."

"Professor Carl Gauss, we want to talk."

"About what?"

"There has been so much death and violence. We want to find a solution that can get this over with as quickly as possible."

"And is it by intruding uninvited into my house that you were thinking to win my trust?"

"That was a... an emergency case."

"What do you mean?"

"We knocked at your door but there was no response, but we had to talk to you before nine."

"Why? What?" A pause, then, "How do you know?"

He looked shocked and his gun's barrel was dwindling nervously. He then looked at the big clock in the room. Its pendulum was slowly swinging from left to right. Eight thirty-nine.

"We know more than you think."

Gauss didn't say anything and kept his gun pointed at them.

"We know that you don't agree with Riemann's... uhm... methods, so to speak. We know that you wanted to talk to us and finish this madness before it's too late."

"How the hell do you know about this? Did you speak with Escher?"

He was sweating and showing signs of panic. His gaze was switching quickly between them and the clock. Nine o'clock was approaching fast. Erwin noticed it and stepped back further with his hands higher than before. He then looked at Marie and Charles, not knowing what to say. If he said anything wrong, Gauss might pull the trigger.

"Did you kill him?" asked Gauss in a shrieking voice.

"No, no, no!" Erwin said, waving his hands in the air.

"Technically not." Charles stepped forward in front of Erwin, triggering Gauss's reaction.

"Move back! Move back!" Gauss shouted.

Charles stepped back, pushing Erwin and Marie closer to the doorstep.

"He is dead now, but we didn't kill him."

"Sure. How convenient to say it now, with me pointing a gun at your face."

"I promise, we didn't kill him. He was involved in a shootout with the army while he was at the portal entrance in his house and..."

"And how do you know this?"

"Because we were there and we saw it. We went through his portal at the university. He left it open and we got into his house. We hid in the loft and..."

"And that's why we know of your opinion on Riemann. We overheard your conversation with Escher," Erwin interrupted Charles.

Gauss lowered the gun by a few degrees. He looked seriously shocked. He probably needed to sit and have a glass of water, but no one had the courage to say it.

"Escher dead," he whispered.

Eight forty-two.

"We want to talk. But we need to do this before Riemann is here. Give us the chance to explain."

Marie stepped into the conversation, and said, "It's just you and Riemann now. You can't rely on Escher anymore as an ally."

Gauss walked back to a chair and threw all his weight onto it. His gun on his lap, he used a white handkerchief to mop the sweat from his forehead. The others relaxed a bit but kept their arms well up in sight.

"I thought I knew him well, that brilliant student I helped mentor. But that Riemann does not exist anymore, substituted by this perverted killing machine. I feared him, so the world should as well."

"We can help," Erwin said.

"Shut up and listen to me," Gauss hissed without looking in his eyes, and with the gun still on his lap pointed at them.

"We don't have much time. He was working on a big weapon. The ultimate weapon, as he liked to call it. That thing that killed most of your kind in Gottingen and made some of you the freaks that you are today was just the beginning. He said he brought it with him in case something would happen, for self-defence. But now I know he wanted to use it anyway and that protest outside the classroom was just a pretext. That weapon was a Tesla coil with the added non-Euclidean formula written on it."

He quickly looked at the clock. Eight forty-nine.

"That day Escher acquired the power to open channels that could connect two distant points in space, like a wormhole as they call them today, right? Riemann couldn't ask for a better power to use. We opened it and got into Tesla's lab in the States. It was at night and Riemann knew exactly where to go and where to find it."

"Find what?"

"The supercoil. A Tesla coil capable of covering tens of kilometres with its radius. An entire city could be powered by one of those things. It was a project paid for by the US military, apparently. And secret, very secret, but Riemann knew about it. If modified with non-Euclidean formulas as what was done with that smaller coil in Gottingen, he could destroy an entire city."

Everyone's mind went back to that accident. It was terrible enough to have experienced the power of that small coil. It was difficult to imagine the sheer force of destruction that the bigger coil could achieve.

"That thing was massive and was on six big wheels, but it was impossible to move. But Riemann had an idea: he asked Escher to open a portal between a railroad close to here and the lab. We hijacked a train and we basically drove it inside the lab. Can you imagine? Hijacked a train, like bandits! Riemann moved and bent the rails at a close distance from the coil by writing non-Euclidean formulas on them. Once the coil was chained to the train he brought it to this side of the world."

He started to laugh with gusto.

"I'm still thinking about Tesla's face when he went into his lab that morning. 'Where is my coil?' He can't still get his head around it, I guess."

"Where is it now?" Marie asked.

"In Riemann's lab, a few hundred metres from here if you want to know. It's a big abandoned warehouse where they were stocking tons of fish for the national market. Still stinking though. Horrible place to do your experiments, if you ask me."

Eight fifty-five.

"He made few modifications but kept it almost untouched. He didn't write his formulas on it this time. He doesn't need that anymore."

He started to tap his forehead with his left index finger.

"He can manipulate reality remotely now through his head."

"He wrote a non-Euclidean formula on his head, we saw it!" Marie almost shouted.

"Yes, that. It was a very degenerate thing to do. But it worked, and he is more powerful than ever. He built a special helmet to rein in its power because it was becoming uncontrollable. You are not going to stop him. Trust me."

"But maybe you can convince him," Erwin said. "You were his mentor, he must listen to you. Escher's influence is over. It's just Riemann and you."

"He won't. His mind is warped like his geometry. He doesn't belong to this world anymore."

Eight fifty-nine.

"But there is one possible way to defeat him. Maybe by writing a Euclidean formula on the coil and using it against him, we have the chance to weaken him and then stop him."

Gong. Everyone startled and looked at the clock.

*Nine o' clock!*

"Do not open the door," Erwin said when he saw Gauss pulling himself up.

"He has the key anyway."

They heard a distant clattering. Keys on metal. Riemann was at the door and getting in.

"He is always sharp. And he never knocks." Gauss started to smile and giggle.

They ignored him, thinking he was going mad.

"What do we do?" asked Marie in a panic.

"We need to hide, then," Erwin said. And then to Gauss: "Pretend nothing has changed and we are not here."

"Sure. Help yourself," Gauss said, slowly opening his arms high to the ceiling like he was encompassing the whole world.

They ran upstairs, hoping he wouldn't find them there. They quickly moved into one of the bedrooms, curtains drawn and lights off.

"What do we do?" Marie asked again in an almost inaudible whisper.

Erwin looked her in the eyes and for the first time that day he touched her face. His hand went to his pale cheek. He could see and feel her veins; she was getting weak.

"No worries. I… I think the best thing is to wait until we find the best chance to get out of here and find that warehouse, and do what Gauss suggested."

"Why don't we go through the loft hatch?" asked Charles, lying on the bed.

"That's an escape route. We don't want to escape. We want to finish this bloody thing once and for all. If we run now the world will be in his clutches and nothing will stop him."

"If that suggestion works though…"

"It's the only thing we've got. It's our only hope."

Their whispers were interrupted by Riemann's footsteps. He walked through the main corridor and stopped where they had left Gauss. It was as if his entrance was enough to strike terror into everyone inside the house.

Erwin, who was closest to the door, could hear someone conversing but didn't understand a single word. He decided to leave the wooden box in the room and crawl out into the corridor. Marie and Charles stayed in the room without protesting.

"Where is Escher?"

"Don't know," Gauss lied. "He should be in anytime now. He is always late, you know."

"Okay, we wait five minutes then we can go."

"Where?"

"I need to show you our little rig."

"Is it finished?" Gauss asked with a mix of excitement and disbelief.

"Patience, my friend, all in due time. You will see with your own eyes."

There was a long pause. Erwin hoped Gauss wasn't betraying them.

"Your helmet. It seems like it is working now."

Riemann didn't reply.

Silence.

Erwin stopped his breath.

"Ehm… the helmet looks nice on you, I have to say."

*Gauss, such a bad actor*, thought Erwin. *He sold us.*

Remarkably, the silence remained in the house even when the floorboards started to roll over Erwin's body. No cracking, no crashing. Not even when his wood-wrapped body was pulled down to the ground floor.

*He managed to manipulate matter and sound! Marie and Charles will never know.*

The fall was painful, and for a few seconds he couldn't breathe. When he finally inhaled dusty air he realised one or more of his ribs were broken. His breaths were short and frequent to avoid putting too much pressure on his ribcage.

He opened his eyes to a slit. The first things he saw were Gauss's and Riemann's shoes, at his eye level.

"Well, well. What do we have here? Someone was eavesdropping uninvited? Didn't your mum tell you…"

A painful bashing on the boards around his body.

"…it's fucking impolite!" Riemann shouted loud, like a madman in a mental institution.

Erwin was now half free from his wooden cage thanks to Riemann's rage, but he didn't dare move. He started to shake and he peed his pants. This time he felt it was over. He thought about Marie and Charles upstairs, unaware of his fate. How terrible the thought of dying without anyone knowing. Apart from your killer, of course.

"I particularly dislike spies, just to let you know."

He was aching all over his body and couldn't focus on what he was saying. He just perceived the furious tone and some of the movements happening in the room from the corner of his eye. At some point Gauss moved away or left the room, from what he could make out.

***

"It's been too long now." Charles said, standing up painfully from the bed.

Marie walked to the door and had a quick peek. Erwin wasn't in the corridor anymore. He must have crawled closer to the stairs. She went down on all fours and slowly pushed herself forward. She pushed and pushed until her hands felt a cut on the floor. She couldn't believe her eyes when her head dropped into a hole in the floor the size of a sofa. Erwin's body was lying on the floor below, immobilised by the boards that were curling around him like a cage. Riemann and Gauss were standing next to him. She heard Riemann shouting at him. About Erwin being a spy, about his lack of gratitude and other nonsense accusations. Erwin didn't move a single muscle and Marie thought the worst.

*Or maybe it is better if he is dead already, so he will be spared all the pain,* she thought.

"And I guess you are not alone. Where are they?

"Erwin Schrodinger. I condemn you to death by non-Euclidean geometry."

Erwin felt something crawling down his spine. And pain. A lot of pain. Then, when he thought he was going to break like a wooden stick in the hands of a giant, he felt relief. It was like being filled up with a warm substance. He was a vessel and pleased to be one.

He couldn't see what was happening to his body.

Marie could do nothing. Something inside told her to jump down and help him, but she was so weak and maybe too fatalistic to think she could do anything more useful that what she was doing now, which was watching. She was going to be dead soon anyway, because of her internal death-clock or because of Riemann. Erwin was a dead man too. If she could call that *thing* a man anymore. Charles wouldn't be able to escape his fate too. Death was among them and they accepted it as normal. Like Erwin, they all felt like vessels, tools to be filled.

69

***

Far away voices, muffled not by distance but by anaesthetised senses. It was as if she was in a bubble, quick glimpses of light coming through her eyelids, her mind detached from her body. Did she have a body still? Is this what death was like? If it was, she was pleased with it. After all the pain, after all that she saw. But she couldn't recall a single episode or faces or a logical sequence of facts now. She knew something bad happened to her and to the people she cared about, but now it was all so distant in time and space.

At first a humming-like sound filled her head, a heartbeat – hers? – that throbbed against her eardrums. Then she heard his dark voice.

"Where is Escher!" Riemann shouted at Gauss.

"He is dead."

"What?"

"They said he died in a shootout with the army because he left one of his chann..."

"And why did you lie to me earlier?"

"I was going to but..."

"But you were too busy conspiring with them?"

And then something cruel happened to Gauss but the whole scene was wrapped in silence, like the room was suddenly in a vacuum. That triggered her memories and she recalled Erwin's body. His mutilations, his impossibly curved limbs, his hyperbolic, newly acquired deformities. Horrible vistas that could have prompted her nausea but didn't. Again, her fatalism negated even that simple human reaction.

## Chapter 7
## Captive

When she woke up, Charles's beard was tickling her ankle. Her body was lying on cold metal and she felt a great weight on her legs. It took her some time to realise that the weight was Charles's head. She pulled herself up and moved it delicately to the floor. He was snoring and the cyclic heavy breathing wasn't minimally perturbed by the change of position.

The room where they were kept captive was made of metal and measured four by two metres. It looked like an old container. Light was pouring in through several holes in the ceiling like a giant colander. The smell, that putrid smell that was permeating their lungs and even their clothes, was coming from those holes. Even Tabby, now was sitting next to Charles, had a rose scent compared to that foul odour. The cat's figure was flickering between its live and dead forms while it was licking its paws. Still Marie couldn't get used to that freakish creature. She shivered.

She was still feeling weak, her head pounding like after a bad hangover. She knew where they were: Gauss had talked about an old warehouse where they processed or stored fish. That's where that smell was coming from. More difficult to understand, though, was the reason why they were still alive and kept prisoners in that container. All that she saw and experienced was just a dream? Erwin's death? Gauss's similar fate? Her body floating in a bubble? Her sense anesthetised in a vacuum? Were they real? Then she saw Charles but not Erwin, and she knew. Still weak, but

71

somehow she awoke less pessimistic than before. While earlier she hadn't cared about her life – being alive or dead were equally irrelevant to her – now a spark of hope came through her veins. She wanted to find a way out of this container. She wanted to escape. She wanted to live.

"I suspect he kept us alive for some sort of experiment. On us, I mean."

Charles's voice broke the silence. His words were barely audible. He seemed tired, powerless.

"We have to get out," Marie responded.

"The only way out is our demise."

"I thought the same before but we can't quit now. We are still in time to stop him."

"And save yourself?"

"No, but we can save thousands or millions of people."

"It's over. No need to prove that we are heroes. We are not."

Marie knew Charles was useless in this state of mind. She stood up and started to search for an opening. The light was dim, but her eyes were getting used to the darkness. No sound was coming from outside, and apart from the overwhelming stench there was no suggestion that their container was inside a bigger building.

She tried to open the main door of the container but it seemed there was a long bar on the other side preventing the door from opening. She decided to give up on that and started to search for another opening, if there was any. She used her fingers to feel for an opening in the metal sheet. She found a small panel for ventilation large enough to get a head through. A small head. But not the rest of the body.

She sighed loudly and slid her back along the metal until she sat on the floor again. In front of her the cat was staring at her while it licked its paws. Next to it the relaxed body of Charles, still with his eyelids closed.

"Given up already?"

"No," she said, standing up again.

She wanted to know where the container was, and what was outside. She focused her mind and placed her hands on the metal. Then she punched it several times, gritting her teeth.

"I cannot see," Marie said.

"What?"

"I can't see through the walls. This container's walls must be made of or covered with lead."

"He must have known of your powers, then."

"That bastard! I can't believe he killed his own mentor. The person that ultimately didn't betray him, even though he didn't agree with his methods."

"What?" This time Charles opened his eyes and turned his face.

"After Erwin's death something happened to me. I'm not sure what exactly. One moment I was peering down at Erwin's body, the next I felt weightless. It was like I was wrapped inside some sort of bubble. I could barely hear any sound and feel any... anything really. Then I saw him killing Gauss with his powers."

"I didn't expect that at all. So he is alone now."

"Most likely."

Marie sighed and sat again on the floor.

"Erwin. He was a good man."

"All men are after they die. With this, I'm not saying he wasn't. It's just..."

"I know, we always say the same words about anyone who leaves us. But I truly think he was a decent man. Too bad the only two people who knew how brave and good he was will be dead soon as well, without telling the world about him."

And after a pause: "I'm not crying. I want to cry but I have no strength to do it."

"Maybe because we are as doomed as him, so we do not feel his loss. The dead do not envy the dead. And besides, all our powers did nothing to save Erwin. They are useless. Even worse, they are a curse."

"No, they aren't. If there is one thing Erwin taught me, it is that our powers are gifts, not curses. It's on us to decide how to use them."

Charles was surprised by her sudden change of mood. She seemed more relaxed, almost like when you remember your dead with a smile after weeks and weeks of mourning. She had accepted his death gently and without scars.

"I'm grateful to Erwin for teaching me this. The first day I met him, he gave me a Superman comic book. We were at

73

the theatre, he said that to me and then gave me the comic, saying that we will meet again. That night I told Pierre I was going to throw that comic away. I think Pierre understood that Erwin fancied me, so I didn't want to create useless jealousies. But I didn't, and I read it that night. Superman's story sounds so familiar to me now. He has to disguise his real identity from everyone, even from his girlfriend, and you might think it is a curse. To hide, to disguise, to lie, to be left alone; a superbeing among billions of inferior beings. Nevertheless, Superman continues to use his powers for the good, for the common good. Despite sometimes feeling the harsh words of the other humans against him. That is how I think a god must feel. Continuously summoned by lesser creatures for futile favours, but then forgotten and often despised. Alone."

"Are you saying we are like gods?"

"No, or perhaps not yet. Not, at least, until we have followers. What I'm trying to say is that the Gottingen Accident took us apart from humanity and put us on another plane of existence. You can create things and I can destroy things. We are not humans anymore, Charles."

"We are not invincible and we can die. And this situation in the container proves it."

"But so are gods. They have died in their thousands since humanity's dawn. And what Nietzsche said recently? *Gott ist tot.*"

"I'm afraid I'm not familiar with Nietzsche."

"Do you think every now and then a Gottingen Accident-type event creates superbeings, which humans then revere as gods? What if we are not the first or the last?"

"Well, I thought about this by applying my theory on what just happened: changes and mutations occurred, natural selection eliminated most of us and only a few survived."

"Why us?"

"Randomness plays a big role in natural selection. Or maybe our powers didn't involve any self-destructing effect on our bodies and kept us alive."

Marie made a face that resembled a sarcastic smile, but was shadowed by sadness.

74

"So what happens after natural selection has killed most of us?"

"Well, it is actually not that straightforward. It's not about killing, it's about offspring production. You see, your mutation is a singularity in time and space that doesn't mean anything in the greater scheme of evolution. You have to transmit your change... ehm gift, to an offspring to keep it in the population. And your offspring needs to survive and reproduce successfully."

"But I'm too old for this."

"Then your gift will die with you and evolution won't see your fantastic powers spread in the population. You are a one-off Superwoman."

"Perhaps a good thing, then. Imagine a world where everyone is a Superman. What would they use their powers for?"

"*In a mad world only the mad are sane*, a Japanese sage said once. They would just be called men, I guess. The few remaining men without powers, on the other hand, would be called..."

"Inferior. Or lesser beings."

"Yes, exactly."

"Maybe you should have given him those gecko feet he wanted. Or that chameleon tongue. Chameleonman, a name for a comic."

"Such a surreal conversation we are having in this situation."

"Conversations like this help..."

"...distracting us from the thought of death."

"Exactly."

"But they don't. To what death are we destined, do you think?"

"He is a sadist. And full of ideas."

"I can think of many deaths, but not any in which I truly die at the hands of someone. Maybe because I'm doomed anyway."

Charles looked at her, puzzled.

"Oh come on, can't you see that my hours are numbered anyway? I'm dying, Charles. Regardless of Riemann, I'm finished."

"So your gift became a curse." Charles managed to spin that otherwise sarcastic sentence into something soft and neutral.

"Only because I chose to. I could have stopped using my powers as I knew they were devouring me. But I chose to give meaning to this life. I gave death to my beloved husband and now to myself, but I tried to save the world in the meantime. But how hollow these words are now that no one else is here listening."

"I am," Charles said. "Not for long, I guess."

They kept quiet for a while and Charles – incredibly, as only old people can – managed to have a nap as well.

Marie's mind flew to other pastures. To her previous life, everyday life. *Why previous?* she asked herself. Did it mean she couldn't go back to her life prior to this turned-sour adventure? For one thing, she was dying and there was no reason to deny this to herself. And it seemed like Charles understood that too. Then, she had lost her husband. Strangely, Pierre wasn't appearing that much in her thoughts, maybe for the same reason why she considered *that* life to be over. That chapter was gone. A new one had opened for few days and now it would be the epilogue.

"It was me that killed him, you know that."

Was it meant as a question or as a statement?

At first Charles didn't reply, but Marie knew he had heard her.

"Wasn't you."

"It was, Charles. You only know what I told you."

"That by accident you put your hands on him and that was enough to kill him. What more is there to say?"

He was trying to minimise her involvement in his death, lessening her guilt.

"That night we'd had an argument. A serious one, violent even. I went to bed still dressed in anger in my heart. He didn't follow me into the bedroom. He probably slept on the couch. I slept the heaviest of nights, and the dream I had was like a continuation of that evening. We were still arguing, shouting. There was a fury in me that I couldn't stop, and I didn't know why it was directed against him. It was all triggered by something frivolous. I didn't like his tone of voice when he mentioned Erwin's story again. He was jealous, of course, but thinking about it now it seemed so natural and harmless. Blood rushed to my head and I felt my hands burning like furnaces. I felt the urge to punish him, something took hold of my brain and focused all the frustration of those days after the accident onto him. I punched him and shoved him to the wall with a strength I didn't know I had. He was in shock and left without the time to think what was happening. I suspect he thought it was going to be a temporary release of anger after all that had happened to me, so he waited punch after punch, kick after kick. But then, fuelled by this unknown rage I punched him even harder, until he lost his senses. My hands went straight to his neck, now without his arms to protect it."

"But it was just a dream."

"I woke up with the sheets in flame, the curtains ablaze with violet-tinged tongues of fire. My clothes, ashes floating in the vortex of the smoke. His screams of pain accompanied that vision of hell. He died with my hands around his neck. Somehow, my dream crossed the border with reality and when he came into the bedroom to save me from the fire I grabbed him and kept him with me. That fire didn't burn my skin but it destroyed everything else around me. And that included my husband. My Pierre."

Her tears were rivers on her cheeks. Charles didn't say anything, nor tried to console her. He knew she had been keeping this inside her for weeks and this was the first time she had told anyone. She cried and cried until she could cry no more and it became a tranquil sobbing. She mopped her face with the sleeve of her shirt and opened her eyes for the first time in a while.

"And you. Why are you staring at me all the time like that?" she shouted at Tabby.

"You have been completely useless, all the time. Why don't you do something like climbing up to that ventilation opening and tell us where we are?"

Tabby stopped licking its paw and looked at the opening she'd mentioned. Then it walked towards it and jumped up onto the short ledge in front of it. Its dead form flickered many times during this, and now its dead body was hanging from the ledge like a towel on a bathroom rail.

Marie didn't say a single thing and she waited for Charles to say something, but nothing came out of his mouth either.

"Tabby, jump down and touch Charles's foot," she said calmly.

Tabby jumped down and touched Charles's left foot with its paw.

"You understand us. You have understood us all this time!"

Marie's mouth remained open for a while and her hand was trying to find a way out of her hair, which was tied in a bundle.

"The Gottingen Accident. It must have mutated its brain too. It brought it consciousness."

"Not so fast. Consciousness is different from understanding simple commands. You can teach any pet to do different tricks."

Charles stood up in excitement.

"Easy to test."

He ducked to the cat's level.

"Tabby, if you are aware of your intelligence can you raise your left paw please?"

Tabby didn't move for a whole minute. Charles sighed in disappointment.

"Maybe it doesn't understand the meaning of complex words like *intelligence* and *consciousness*," Charles said, turning his face to Marie.

But Marie didn't even pay attention to his words and was pointing at the cat, her finger quivering and her mouth wide open.

Tabby's left paw was up.

"Mother of God."

Charles threw himself back and landed on the floor.

"Hey, if that's so, let's ask it to get out of here and seek help," Marie said with a newly acquired excitement.

"How can it seek and ask for help when it doesn't speak?"

"Yes, good point."

"Unless it has the vocal cords."

Charles smiled, knowing how foolish he probably sounded.

"What?" Marie almost shrieked.

"Think about it: you can give it a command, but it won't be able to communicate the results to us. Or if you are asking it to get help, how can it even try?"

"It seems crazy to me," Marie said, with a tone that was alluding to a permissive change her mind.

"And Broca's area, the area of the brain responsible for speech. And possibly a slight modification of the lips."

"Are you sure you can do all this?"

Tabby quickly moved away from them. Marie followed it from the corner of her eye.

"This is going to be completely different from what I've done in the past. Almost of a surgical precision."

Marie stopped him and pointed at his back. "The only issue is that Tabby understood everything you said, and it seems unhappy about it."

They both looked at the cat, which was now hiding in the darkest corner, back to the metal. Ears were low and hairs were up. Its dead form was lying on the floor unperturbed.

"Look Tabby: this is not going to hurt you," Charles started. "It will actually improve your already extraordinary skills to a new, higher level. Think about it: you will be able to communicate with us and with anyone else you would like to."

There was a meow that went up in tone for a few seconds. During this feline crescendo its fangs became visible and Charles swore he even saw its claws coming out of the paws. It wasn't going to be that easy.

"We've fought against worse foes than this. A couple of scratches are nothing compared to what we've passed through," said an infuriated Marie, launching herself forward to catch Tabby.

The cat jumped up a metre or so, avoiding her clutches. When she tried to get it again its claws went into action and she received two deep scratches on her right hand.

"Tabby, you are making this worse. Calm down and everything will be okay." Charles was shouting like someone watching a fight in an arena.

Marie managed to catch it, but only when it was in its dead form. She felt its soft body full of pus but she kept hold of it nonetheless. When the alive form came up, though, things changed quickly. Its limbs were in a different position compared to the dead form. It tried to scratch at her eye level, so she had to let it loose. Charles moved forward to help.

"Get it when it's alive!" she shouted.

With a lot of luck Charles managed to grab it, after it jumped a metre forward and landed in his arms. He held it by its torso and let Marie hold the legs.

"Do it now!"

Charles closed his eyes and pulled his head back as if in a trance state. Tabby stopped moving and its eyes narrowed down to a slit too. You could see some of the white of the eye on both. Marie relaxed her hold a little, feeling that the cat wasn't going to fight back anymore. She waited and waited until she heard Charles mumbling something. His forehead creased in concentration. Strangely, the dead form didn't appear at all during this, almost as if its quantum abilities were temporarily lost. She asked herself how he was able to focus his powers on a specific body area. How to find the throat, the larynx? How to find the right place and make the right connection in the brain?

***

The first time she had seen his head in that trance-like position was in his lab, a few days after that moment in her kitchen when he had told her about his powers and she had found out about hers. He had discovered his powers on his finches, and for weeks he had managed to change or deform – depending on how you saw it – all his birds. When he'd finished them he'd bought another batch because he wanted to experiment on as many as possible.

"I wrote to Wallace. He is still in Indonesia. I asked him to send me some of the monkeys he is studying in the wild now. Zoos in Europe don't want to send me any specimens."

80

"Well, it's understandable. You are going to send them back deformed and unrecognisable."

Charles shook his head, clearly not understanding her sarcasm. "They don't know what I'm capable of. Yet."

He wanted to show her his collection before he could move on to a live experiment on the new batch. The cages were in a conservatory at his house which faced south. There were hundreds of them from different species. Most of them were from Galapagos islands. When originally caught they had been differentiated from each other by size, plumage, the shape of the beaks and other minor features. Now their differences were ranging from additional fingers to legs, wings, heads. Eyes were opening anywhere in their bodies but their heads. Some were undisturbed by their new features, but others were obviously in pain. What had started as a fascinating tour of a Victorian cabinet of curiosities ended up being a descent to a macabre show played in a dungeon.

She felt extremely moved by those sights, and she tasted some sickness in her mouth.

"You should at least sacrifice some of them."

"What do you mean?"

"The pain. I can see some of them are not happy with their new... assembly."

"Maybe I should ask for help from Konrad Lorenz."

He dropped that sentence without any hint of emotion. Was he sarcastic or did he really mean it?

He moved to the cage where the new batch was kept. Before he opened the cage he looked into Marie's eyes and said: "I did terrible things to some of them and I'm not proud of that, but I always end their pain if they suffer."

*Meaning that the ones that are here are only the ones that survived the first selection? How many didn't, though?*

"I'm improving in my mutation skills and fewer and fewer are coming out with deformities. The only way for me to improve is to try it on some more. The future benefits for the science, and even for themselves, are greater than few dead ones."

"Ends don't justify the means, you know that," she said with an angry tone.

"Come with me," he said, leaving the cage he was opening behind them.

They went to another room adjacent to the conservatory. In a recess that once could have been used as a cupboard there was a roosting chicken in a big cage. She'd grown used to the bird-dropping smell, but here it was more pungent.

"One day a local peasant brought her to me. He said he was going to kill her because of a deformation on her neck. He thought it was better to give it to me for experiments, as he didn't trust a 'cursed chicken', so he told me. The cursed chicken happened to have a tumour on her neck. A big, fatty ball that prevented her swallowing. She was condemned. A week? Give or take."

"But I see nothing on her..." Marie stopped abruptly, knowing how stupid she must have sounded.

Charles casually fed the chicken some corn.

"Okay, I see where you want to go with this but..."

Charles ignored her and moved back to the conservatory. Marie followed him, almost begging for attention.

"Okay, I admit it. What you have done to the chicken is a miracle and I wish you could bring a better future for all of us, including other animals but..."

"Marie, I have to refine my skills so that one day I can get better and target the right area without damaging the specimen or the person. There is nothing you can say that can change my mind. Now, help me with this new bird."

He took a finch out of the cage and asked her to hold it while he was concentrating. Marie didn't really want to be in that position. She was still moved by what she had seen, disgusted even; she understood his motives and logic but wished she had more time to digest it all. And because of this she wasn't really surprised to see her body's reaction: her hands were glowing like furnaces.

*No, not again!*

She thought she was going to kill the bird and hurt Charles. But he had his eyes closed and no words came out of her mouth. To her surprise, the bird didn't flinch and neither did Charles.

Was she able to irradiate without hurting them? She couldn't believe her eyes.

When Charles woke from his trance the bird, still in Marie's glowing-red hands, was displaying a much bigger body, with a wonderful multicolour plumage, a longer beak and a long tail.

"I can't believe it!" Charles shouted. "I made it. It came out exactly as I thought it would!"

And then, looking at her hands: "Your hands. What happened to your hands?"

"Sorry, I can't control it really. I thought I was going to kill it and hurt you, but I didn't. How is that possible, Charles?"

"Hang on," he said, putting the still asleep bird in the cage and taking another bird. "Try again with this one."

They did it, and again the mutations were exactly as Charles predicted.

"Your hands. Your hands are helping me to focus my skills. It's like you are accelerating the rate of mutations with your X-rays." And holding her glowing hands without fear of getting hurt: "We can join forces!"

They tried several more times with extraordinary results, and that cabinet of horrors was starting to look more like an Eden full of wonderful creatures. But Eden is not forever and disaster struck. Once Marie, perhaps tired, lost control of her powers and a bird burned to ashes, Charles got hurt and jumped back, hitting his back on a desk quite badly. She fainted soon after. Her last memory was of the shrieks of pain from the little finch still echoing on her mind.

*** 

In what it felt like hours, but in fact were mere minutes, Charles recovered from his trance state and went down like a sack of potatoes. She was left with Tabby in her hands. The dead form was back but for the first time dead and alive bodies were in the same position: both lying, one dead and the other asleep.

"I hope I didn't kill it," Charles murmured while still on the floor.

"Yes, if the dead can still snore. And don't forget that it is already dead. Well, partially. Do I have to remind you that as a quantum cat, it's both alive and dead at the same time?"

"Mmff." Charles dismissed the conversation, too tired to talk after all the energy he had put into it.

"Shall we wake it up?"

Charles shrugged and said nothing, sitting on the floor with his eyes closed.

Marie placed Tabby on the floor and started to poke it, being careful to do so only when it was alive. It woke up after several pokes and looked confused.

"Can you talk now?" Marie asked.

Tabby stood up in a sitting position and meowed something.

"Talk."

Nothing for several minutes. Some toileting and other typical feline occupations, but no words. Its dead form, though, was appearing with a lower frequency than before. Something had changed in its quantum characteristics.

"Charles, I'm not sure it worked."

"Give it some time. You didn't learn to speak in an hour."

"What? You mean we have to teach it how to speak? It may take years!"

"I believe it may happen sooner than that, as its consciousness is already developed and it understands our language perfectly."

The meowing was becoming less and less recognisable, distorted even. Like a sound coming from scratched vinyl on an old record player. While doing so, Tabby was looking at Marie and Charles with a very human-like expression. It helped that its lips were slightly more visible underneath the fur and the whiskers.

"It's trying to say something!"

"Come on Tabby! You can do it."

The cat was struggling to get something out of its mouth but with no success. Its frustration was growing as much as Marie's and Charles's.

"Come on! Something simple, like your name. Say Ta-ta-ta and then bby-bby-bby."

"Perhaps something closer to the sound of a meow. Your name, Marie! Try it!""

"Yes! Say Ma-ma-ma."

Live Tabby started to posture itself with the neck forward and placed its lips like it was going to say the letter M.

Then, when everyone was excited to hear the first word from a cat's mouth – something that no human being had ever experienced before and which would be written in the history books – the only sound that came out was the unmistakable typical feline sound of a ball of hair being vomited.

"Yuk," said Charles, stepping back from the hair-ball on the floor.

"That's truly disgusting," said Marie. And then: "But I guess it's still a cat after all. What did you expect?"

"I expect respect. That's what I expect," Tabby said out of the blue.

And it surprised everyone, including Tabby itself.

# Chapter 8
## The Old Fishery

I f you are wondering what a surprised facial expression would look like on a cat, look no further than that on a human: eyes wide open, jaws down, still face muscles. And yet to Marie and Charles there was a hint of alien features in it. Those lips, able to mutter human sounds, were freakishly uncomfortable to see.

No one moved for a full minute, until the dead form of the cat appeared again for few seconds. A few seconds in which Marie and Charles looked at each other in disbelief. Charles had made it, and it was the most incredible scientific breakthrough they'd happened to witness, as well as the most disturbing.

"What you have done is despicable. I will never forgive you..." Live Tabby was back and it reappeared with a burst of angry words. It stopped, hearing the sound of its own voice. It must be quite bizarre, hearing your voice – which until then was relegated to your inner self – for the first time.

"And by the way, I'm a *he* not an *it*," he said stubbornly.

Tabby looked at his paws, palms up, like they were the very reason why he could talk. "I can't believe it. Words are coming out of my mouth like you humans do. I was getting used to keep them in my brain, I could understand them, I could understand all of you but I couldn't express myself. And this since that accident in my owner's office. All my brothers dead, weirdly deformed – and I, the only one that survived, am here now talking to you. From the reactions on your faces I'm guessing I'm the first of my kind, a special, unique creature. I have to admit that you, Charles, did a great job. I withdraw my earlier comment and I apologise. What you have done to me is not despicable, it is extraordinarily wonderful!"

Marie rolled her eyes up and placed her palm on her forehead before saying: "That's just perfect. After a three-headed giant dog, now a chatty zombie cat."

Charles decided to ignore her.

"Well, Tabby, you are welcome. And…" he struggled to find the right words. "…and you are also welcome to our world, the world of sentient and talking beings."

"I can't wait to use my newly acquired skills in an academic contest. But first I need to get out of this place."

"And let us out, right?"

Marie couldn't believe Charles was asking that question with a begging tone.

"Absolutely. And that ventilation opening is perfect for my size." And when he'd finished his sentence, the dead form appeared lying on the floor.

The behaviour of the quantum cat was changing in a very unexpected way: the live and dead forms were lasting longer, but the switching frequency was much lower.

"Very interesting indeed. My intervention in his biology must have altered the quantum cycle," Charles mumbled to himself.

Marie took advantage of Tabby's temporary absence.

"How can we use him? Will he kill Riemann with a long convoluted story? Death by boredom?"

Charles looked at her with a frowning forehead.

"Do I have to remind you that Newton saved our lives earlier? And so will Tabby."

Live Tabby must have resurfaced and heard the last sentence, as he quickly replied: "Your likelihood of survival will increase considerably when I'm outside of this room – I mean, container," Tabby said, rolling his head around. "You have to trust my newly acquired abilities. It's your only chance to get out of here alive."

"Well said. I'm starting to like this cat," Charles said with a giggle.

"You will like me even more when I've had the chance to show you what a prodigy of nature I now am."

Marie didn't say anything. She was just too tired. She couldn't believe they were talking to a cat. A cat that had a posh accent and used words out of a Victorian poem, even!

Tabby climbed up onto the small ledge and disappeared out of the container through the ventilation hole.

"And now?"

"And now we wait."

The little cat face came back after a minute.

"I guess you know by now that we are inside a place where they used to process fish. It smells wonderful in here, in fact. At least from a cat's perspective. No sight of people or any other beings, including fish, long dead years ago I guess. There is a huge metal column with a doughnut-shaped top. Never seen anything like that before. There are several containers like this one abandoned in the warehouse. Only ours is locked."

"How?"

"There is a bar that prevents the doors from opening."

"Do you think you can slide it?"

"I can surely try, although my paws are not as advanced as yours for this task. But I'm not sure you would like me to open it though."

"What do you mean?"

"It's difficult to describe, and my vocabulary is limited at the moment, but let's say that in these few days you have grown used to sufficiently weird and crazy things. So this one probably won't disturb you that much. Maybe…"

"What? What are you talking about? What's outside?"

Too late, as the cat's face disappeared from the hole. They heard some rummaging at the doors coming from outside. Then several blows to the metal and then a clang.

"You can push them now," the little feline voice said from outside.

"He did it! I can't believe he did it!" said Charles, throwing all his weight at the metal doors.

Bright light hit them and they had to cover their eyes. It took them a while to slowly adapt to the bright environment. Tabby was there on the dark pavement, lying dead and unresponsive. Most of the light was coming from half-broken windows. It wasn't that bright now that they were used to it. It was actually the light of a sunset. The warehouse was huge, and all they could see around them were empty containers like the one they were kept captive in, all spread across the surface. From one end to the other was probably a hundred metres, but something wasn't right about the walls and the ceiling. At a micro level it looked like a fishery: concrete tanks, a myriad of tubes and a net of plumbing from one tank to the other, cranes, hooks and benches still stained with old blood. The wooden surfaces were scarred by countless cuts. Although it had been shut for years the smell of rotten fish was still permeating the air, possibly because of the fish tanks and benches that were never properly cleaned. It was like the business suddenly went bust and this place was left in a day, as it was during a normal day of work.

But at a macro level the walls were too high and the distances were too long and distorted. It was only when their eyes went up to the ceiling that they realised they were inside another of those weird non-Euclidean environments. This time it wasn't Escherian in taste and that triggered a sigh of relief in both Charles and Marie. But they suddenly realised they were inside another type of bizarre place. There was a city above their heads. Their minds couldn't understand how a city could fit into that warehouse, how a city with Manhattan-style skyscrapers dangling from the top upside-down and huge net of roads and bridges could be on the ceiling. During those days they had grown used to weird epiphanies, but this was surpassing them all. The space was distorted in such a way that at their level the warehouse was still small enough for humans to walk from one side to the other, but when their gaze moved up the space and sizes were beyond their comprehension.

They were dozens of skyscrapers hanging upside-down on the ceiling – or should we call it ground, now? –

and bridges and tunnels connecting them together like in an urban concrete jungle. Their styles ranged from classical to renaissance, from art deco to art nouveau, but the general look was of a futuristic city. Flying cars and rockets departing to the moon wouldn't have been out of place in that environment at all.

Emerging from that space, almost at its centre, was a huge palace made of concrete that was pointing its tall tip towards them. Looking at it made their heads dizzy and they felt like that city was in a precarious stability and could crumble onto them at any minute. Adding to that there was an eerie absence: the city was deserted and there were no people, no cars, no trains or flying cars and rockets. It was like a city built for the purpose of architectural pleasure rather than to live within it. A city-model that emerged from a crazy mind.

"What is this place?" Charles asked in awe.

Marie attempted an explanation, trying in doing so to keep her mind at ease.

"It's an old fishery. At our level at least, but widely and wildly transformed by non-Euclidean shapers to resemble an underground city of some sort up there."

"I told you this was going to be weird," Tabby said, curling his tail and looking up.

"This vaguely reminds me of Piranesi and his 'prisons'. Monumental architecture, massive towers and bridges all interconnected to each other and yet not a single soul in this landscape. Prisons without prisoners. This is a city without citizens."

Next to them, at approximately ten metres, there was a tall metal column with a torus-shaped tip. The Tesla-coil was massive and impressive. There was a machine next to it. Marie walked towards it and touched the many levers, buttons and lights that populated its surface.

"It's a Turing machine. I can't believe I'm touching this."

"What is it?" Tabby asked with an added meow, and jumping onto it.

"It's a mechanical calculator that can do what a man can do hundred times faster and better. I thought I would never see one of these. I thought they were all destroyed when London was reduced to ashes by the German raids during the Great War. Riemann must use this to command the coil."

"Talking about him, where is he now?" asked an apprehensive Charles.

Tabby's last words before his switch to the dead form: "I didn't see any sign of him and heard nothing so far in the..."

Marie and Charles became wary. They realised they had been very incautious since they'd got out of the container. Riemann could have been hiding anywhere and they were talking loudly, exposed to any attack from any point in the warehouse, without any nearby shelter. Very reckless of them. Charles grabbed Tabby's body from the Turing machine and walked close to the container they had escaped from. He invited Marie too. It seemed like a good place to hide with their shoulders protected while thinking about a plan.

"Right. Riemann is not in here, otherwise he would have killed us already. So, we have an advantage over him. He doesn't know we escaped."

"I think we should wait for his return and stop him."

"We can't stop him, Marie. He is too powerful!"

"So, what are you suggesting we do then?"

"We do exactly what Gauss told us to: write a Euclidean formula on the coil before he comes back. Hopefully that will counteract his non-Euclidean powers."

"How can you trust him after what he did to us? He betrayed us."

"It's the only logical way, Marie. You can fight a non-Euclidean shaper with his own weapon, only of an opposite force. I think he was genuinely trying to suggest to us a way of stopping him. He didn't want him to reach this level of... madness!"

"Okay, I guess it doesn't hurt. But we have no chalk, no pencil, no marker with us."

"We are going to scratch it onto the metal surface of the coil. That would do."

Live Tabby came back from the dead, and he immediately said in a very low funereal voice: "He is here."

91

He looked to the far end of the warehouse, where he'd heard his footsteps coming from. Charles stood up and locked the doors of the container with the bar. Hopefully he wouldn't immediately realise they had escaped, and that would give them an advantage over him. They quickly moved to the back of a nearby container, but still with a good view of the coil and the Turing machine. The light was duller now and the container cast a nice shadow on them.

"This will ruin our plans. What do we do?" Charles whispered in Marie's ear.

Marie had frozen in a still position, unable to move a muscle. The look on her face told Charles she was terrorised. Each of Riemann's echoing footsteps in the warehouse was ticking the gauge of her fear further and further. He started to feel the same, and he realised the closer Riemann was coming towards them, the more panic he was feeling. Consciously or unconsciously, Riemann was able not only to bend matter but to shape their emotions as well.

Finally, they saw him, a curved and gnarled figure approaching his machine of mass destruction. The aura of fear that he was projecting was somehow disproportional to his weak and deformed human figure. If you didn't know about his powers, you might have thought he wouldn't put up much of a fight. His head was facing the Turing machine all the time now, so he had turned his back on them. He turned it on and tens of lights went on at the same time. An electrical sound buzzed in their ears, almost like a very high-voltage hum. Was he going to use the weapon now? Right now? Marie hoped not, but she couldn't move or say anything. She felt her knees quivering; she wanted to wee badly but she managed to keep it in and succeeded in not embarrassing herself at such a tragic moment. She knew Charles felt the same terror and – although she knew little about feline behaviour –Tabby as well.

The hum stopped abruptly. Riemann had switched it off. He was probably just testing it before the grand finale. He lifted his head up in a stargazing posture and looked at the city above. The concrete palace was exactly perpendicular to his body. He stood there for minutes with his eyes closed and his chin up, almost like he was trying to connect to the architectural might on top of him. That dreamlike posture made him appear more human. Like a kid waiting for a shooting star in a cloudless night at the beach.

Charles quickly thought that there might have been a purpose in positioning the Tesla coil exactly underneath that huge palace.

*Channelling! The palace is like an antenna and amplifier at the same time!*

He wanted to shout out what he had just uncovered. Tabby looked at him, and in a way for a few moments – albeit incredible, between two different species – he knew that Tabby thought the same.

*We have to move the coil from underneath the tip of the palace. That might not stop the destructive power of the coil, but it would limit it for sure to a few miles' radius.*

He needed to tell the others, but how? The warehouse's absence of sound was eerie. He could hear Riemann's breath from that distance. They couldn't move a single muscle, as it might result in Riemann realising they were there.

Then he suddenly turned towards the container they were held prisoner in. He leaned his head against the metal like he was trying to eavesdrop inside. The expression on his face shifted from curious to suspicious to angry. Only in that moment did both Marie and Charles realise that he wasn't wearing his helmet. The thought of Riemann starting to have his non-Euclidean seizures without the protective helmet sent a shiver down Marie's spine. He banged on the metal doors but heard nothing in return. So he decided to walk around the container, to check whether there was any other opening. He was starting to get frustrated and walked away, closer to the coil. From there he simply focused his eyes for few seconds on the container and squashed it like it was a beer can. A massive five-by-two-metre iron shipping container weighing several tons was crushed in a fraction of a second. The sudden and brutal overreaction shocked them to the bone. They could have still been inside it. His powers had grown massively and now they had no courage to leave their little hiding place.

93

He then inspected the ball of metal, probably hoping to find signs of his prisoners, but he could see nothing. He looked left and right and back towards the coil. He started to run and inspected every single container. Luckily, he started from the one opposite theirs so they still had some time to think about what to do next.

Charles: "He is very pissed off."

Marie: "He will kill us on sight."

Tabby: "I have a plan."

"What?" Marie and Charles asked, almost in unison.

"Briefly, because we haven't much time. He doesn't know about my intellectual properties so it's very unlikely he would consider me a primary target. I'll run towards him, distracting him, while you guys write the Euclidean formula on the coil column."

He then dashed out of the shadows and ran towards him. Riemann was running himself, checking every single container that was lined up in the warehouse. Tabby followed him and quickly moved to one side, squeezing himself between the back of the containers and the wall so that he couldn't see him just yet. When Riemann looked at the last container, next to the warehouse entrance, a high-pitched meowing started to fill the otherwise silent air. Riemann stopped and waited.

Tabby jumped out from behind the container and landed on its top. He was meowing and waving his long tail, and while doing so moving towards Riemann. Riemann didn't react, not even when Tabby jumped down and started to purr.

Charles and Marie moved quickly out of their hiding spot and reached the coil. The massive column was big enough to cover them from Riemann's sight. Marie picked a hairpin from her hair and started to scribble a formula on the metal surface. It was working, but it was tedious and her hands were sweating. She was almost finished when from the corner of her eye she caught an unusual movement on the wall next to them. She tried to focus on the scribbling as much as she could, but she couldn't help recognising a familiar shape. The wall was moving, like something or someone was inside it or *part of it* – difficult to describe – and she swore she recognised that shape but her brain hadn't enough courage to admit it. Charles realised Marie was distracted by something and he hissed in her ear: "What are you waiting for? Riemann could be back any time soon!"

The distant meowing and the metal-on-metal scratching were enough to drive him mad, but what he saw on the wall, overlooking Marie's head, froze him. He recognised what was on the wall but couldn't express it with words. He wanted to puke, but instead his mouth produced a cry. The wall had two hands waving in the air, and the best way to describe it was like a body imprisoned behind a silicone sheet trying to escape from it. The rest of the body was a collage of non-Euclidean geometrical shapes. The torso was twisted, legs were split and curved backward, the breast was unnaturally inward-shaped in a collection of non-Euclidean paraphernalia. The face, though, that was still recognisable. That nose, that forehead, those eyes, albeit not following Euclidean geometry, were still his, for what they were looking at and being shocked by was Erwin's body imprisoned in the wall.

"Erwin," Charles muttered.

Marie dropped the hairpin from the shock. Charles bent down, searching for it, but the floor was dark so it took him a while to find it; and when he found it underneath the plinth of the Tesla coil he saw Riemann coming towards them. Tabby was still meowing and walking through his legs as only cats can do. Tabby was still alive though, which was very unlikely given the circumstances. Charles wouldn't have bet on it. Riemann was now walking faster, like he suspected something was happening behind the coil. He found Tabby distracting and annoying now, and decided to kick him, throwing him towards the wall. Tabby looked dead, although Charles wasn't sure whether he'd switched to his dead form in the air or not.

"Marie, you have to finish the formula, Riemann is coming and he looks pretty pissed off."

Marie wasn't listening. He saw her touching Erwin's hand, almost like she was seeing a ghost. Erwin was still alive but in a cruel and corrupted shell. She couldn't believe her eyes. She wanted to free him from the wall but it seemed like he was part of it. Erwin looked her in the eyes and it was like he was speaking of pain, sorrow and desperation. She wondered if their fate was supposed to be the same as his. Why imprison them in the container when Riemann could have killed them immediately, then? He wanted to experiment on them, probably hoping to create a weapon out of their powers. A weapon that he could have commanded, bending their wills the same way he was able to bend matter. He probably didn't know that Erwin didn't inherit any power from the Gottingen Accident. So he simply froze him in the wall like a macabre piece of furniture.

The flow of her thoughts was stopped when Charles put the hairpin in her hand and screamed to her. He was saying that the formula was still unfinished and that Riemann had found them and was running towards them. She woke up and bent to her knees to continue scribbling. She saw Charles running away from the cover of the coil, and she understood that he was trying to be a decoy, so she could have more time. An anisotropic wave followed him and missed him by few centimetres. Riemann was without his helmet and his head was exploding with non-Euclidean fury. Charles found refuge behind a container but Riemann crushed it like he did before with the one they were kept in. Charles jumped back and hid behind another one. Again, that was crushed like a tin beneath a boot.

Marie knew she hadn't much time, but the more disturbing thing was that she had doubts about the formula she was writing. Was it right? It had been a long time since her geometry course, and to be perfectly honest it wasn't her favourite subject either. She stopped panicking about the fact that the ending might be wrong.

"I can't be sure about this!" she said in a loud voice.

"Do it!" she heard Charles shouting, while he was taking cover behind the containers.

"What should I do? If it's wrong that's over, we can't correct it anymore," she whispered to herself, while drops of sweat streamed down her forehead.

"Marie." A distant voice, as if from the bottom of a well.

*It can't be,* she thought.

She turned to the wall and saw Erwin bending towards her, inviting her to come closer.

"Marie." Another invitation, like a whisper from a distant corridor.

She stood up and leaned her face towards his. It took a long time – or at least, this what her mind thought – and although she saw Charles almost being crushed multiple times, she stood next to the wall listening. She saw Tabby coming back to his alive form and jumping onto Riemann's head now. Another anisotropic wave and Charles could have been killed and transformed into a wrinkled piece of flesh. Charles stopped running, out of breath, not believing his luck. Saved again by a pet. His hands on his knees, he looked at Marie. She waved her hands.

"I got it!" she yelled.

She finished the formula and started to run towards him. She grabbed his hand and pulled him towards the entrance of the warehouse.

"We need to get out of here, now!"

Charles looked back at the scene they were leaving behind. Tabby was on top of Riemann's head and was furiously scratching at his face. Riemann was grizzling, trying to get him off of his face.

"Tabby!"

"Tabby is able to look after himself pretty well. Remember, he is kind of immortal."

They ran as quickly as they could and they got out of the warehouse in a matter of seconds. It was night now and the roads were deserted. But even if they had encountered anyone, it wasn't going to be any help against Riemann. Charles was out of breath again and couldn't run anymore. He tripped, pulling Marie down with him.

"It's not over, Charles. He is still able to kill."

"I can't run, Marie. I'm too old for this. It's a miracle I avoided all of his waves earlier."

She pulled his body along the deserted street but her adrenaline was depleting quickly and she felt weak again. She sat next to him, her arms down in a gesture typical of someone giving up.

"He helped us, Charles."

"Who?"

She stopped pronouncing his name. She couldn't believe what had just happened in the warehouse. His voice, a thousand miles away and yet so close. She felt something, she felt like someone had hacked her mind. An opening, a channel through the wall. He opened a gate from his mind to hers. He didn't whisper the words, like the ones we primitively shaped with our lips. It was a projection of images and feelings. He told her the exact formula to scribble, but with it he also gave her the opportunity to navigate in his mind. In the beginning she was scared. In what it felt like hours, she then slowly let it go. She went in and it was like walking fully dressed in a giant puddle, dark water up to her chest. Nowhere to go but a small, dull dot on the horizon. She followed it and she saw his pain. She saw what had happened to him, what that evil being that they called Riemann did to him. It wasn't about body parts being dislocated or warped that shocked her. It was more about what had happened to his mind. When the laws of physics are changed it's easy to see what happened to the matter, but what about the mind? What happens to your thoughts when non-Euclidean geometry gets into your head? Are thoughts linear as before? Does effect B descend from cause A? Is A distinct from B or are they indistinguishable? Is 2+2=4 always correct or does it depend on other factors? Factors that are completely out of your control. The world doesn't follow your mind templates. Non-Euclidean minds are not paired with reality. They are lost, rogues without aim or principles. Ghosts that wander the earth within another plane of existence.

She saw that and she felt it and immediately found it repulsive. Her mind started to warp, contaminated by non-Euclidean perversity. She tried to keep steady, to hold an umbilical cord to the real world by thinking about Pierre, her loving Pierre. She tried to remember him while he was smiling rather than when she killed him on that unfortunate night. It was reassuring to have an anchor like him in her mind, he kept her afloat while she was scanning Erwin's mind to find the clues to what had happened. She saw him being transported in a bubble similar to the one she was cocooned in earlier, before she woke up in the container. He was kept still and buoyant for hours until he found himself – or at least, the non-Euclidean version of himself – in the warehouse. She saw with his eyes that he had been chained to the wall. In front of him tens of metal containers and the Tesla coil. He then, after what felt like days, watched other bubbles being chaperoned into the warehouse. She recognised herself and Charles and Tabby unconscious, being locked in one of the containers.

Then he saw Riemann dragging what appeared to be a limping and beaten Gauss. They argued for minutes, with Riemann waving his index finger at him like an inquisitor would do to a heretic. He watched Riemann doing to Gauss what he did to him earlier. It had been a bestial reaction, out of the blue, and took Gauss by surprise. Erwin relived his pain again but through the pain of someone else. And Marie with him, now that she was navigating through his memories. Gauss was the first to be buried within the wall of the warehouse next to Erwin. Then it was going to be Erwin's turn. It was clear that Marie, Charles and Tabby were going to be the next ones to be added to his collection.

Was he dead or alive? How could he feed himself? How could he breathe? How could his body survive embedded within inorganic material? She knew what the answer was but she couldn't express it with words. The only thing she could do was find a metaphor for it. While we walk on the sand, we leave behind our footprints. These are not part of ourselves but they represent us. So it was the same with Erwin: that was a footprint of him, as on a sandy beach. A footprint with a consciousness.

***

She realised she was still, and with her mouth opened in the cold of the night. Charles was still waiting.

"Erwin. He whispered the correct formula to me. I wasn't sure about it but he helped me out. He could speak, barely speak behind that wall – and by the way, they were not spoken words like between me and you now – and he used all his energy to help us. It must have been very painful for him."

"Do you think we can still save him?"

Her answer was silent. Charles felt shivers down his spine.

The doors of the warehouse were still open and they could see inside. Riemann still battling against Tabby and behind them the massive structure of the coil. They didn't know how long they had. They had no plan B. The coil was probably non-functional now. At least from a non-Euclidean point of view. It was clear to both of them that the fate of Erwin was still haunting their minds. They didn't want to be the next ones for Riemann to experiment on. They felt powerless though. A long and hard adventure coming to an end.

Tabby dropped dead again and Riemann found himself free but confused. What happened to that cat? One moment it was scratching his face, a moment later it was dead. He kicked it ferociously again. It took him some time to recover, his face all wounded with bloody cuts. He went straight to the coil rather than searching for Marie and Charles. He clearly wanted to finish this, once and for all. He activated the Turing machine and gave maximum power to the coil. The air around it started to fill with sparkles. They heard it from a distance: the sizzling in the air and that smell of ozone were unmistakable.

Then he pushed a button and the coil funnelled all its energy up towards the top of the upside-down palace in the ceiling. They saw a beam of sparkling light going up, but they couldn't see the end as the frame of the door would not allow them to see the ceiling. They waited, Marie with her fingers crossed, hoping the formula would work.

Something might have gone wrong, very wrong, because they first heard Riemann screaming, then they saw him running away from the coil. Faster and faster until he reached the doors and jumped forward, before the whole warehouse collapsed. The last thing they saw was the top of the massive palace precipitating against the coil. The whole city had collapsed, and with it the warehouse. The energy of the coil, now of Euclidean nature, had destroyed the very fabric of the non-Euclidean city. How a massive metropolis had crumbled within the limited space of the warehouse was a mystery, as much as its very existence. A cloud of dust and debris came towards them as a wave. Marie instinctively covered Charles's body and she closed her mouth and eyes. The smell was of dirt, and thick. A

100

shower of small debris fell on them after a few seconds of calm. A roof panel nearly hit them. Several minutes later, the dust had settled and the road was now full of people in their pyjamas. And after a few minutes, more and more people were rushing towards the scene. A woman still in her robe ran towards them and asked: "Are you alright?"

Marie tried to stand up and a couple of men arrived to help her. Charles was unconscious but still alive. They were completely covered in grey dust and the unknown woman tried to clean Marie's face as best she could. Some others were starting to dig inside the debris in search of survivors.

"No, don't do it!" she said, leaning with all her body and her arm stretched out.

They looked at her like she was crazy. Why not search for other survivors? She must be still in shock, their gazes said to each other.

"No worries. They will take care of that," said a bearded man who looked vaguely like a doctor. "Are there any others under the rubble? What happened, by the way?"

She said *no* with her head. "No one else. Just me and Charles. And Tabby of course."

"Who is Tabby?"

"Our cat."

"Are you sure? You look pretty shocked. The police and the ambulance will be here any minute."

Charles was now being taken care of by two men. She moved close to him and took his hand. His beard and hair were covered in soot. He looked at her with a big question mark on his face.

"Is he…?" he whispered so the others couldn't hear.

"Dead? Not sure Charles. Not sure."

And then, after a while: "We need to stop them digging. I have a bad feeling about it."

Several men were digging with shovels. Some kids arrived with buckets and pails so they could remove the rubble far away.

"No one would believe you, Marie."

"I know but…"

Blue lights started to appear at the far end of the road. People moved away from the middle of it. Two nurses came out of an ambulance bringing a stretcher. They asked many questions, but they received few answers. People were gathering around them so it took a policeman to spread them away. The police asked many questions too, but Marie and Charles didn't give away anything. Who would have believed them?

Then Marie had an idea.

"I need to talk to Police Chief Schmidtz, now."

One of the policemen waved his hand like it was out of the question.

"He knows us and knows about what happened here," Marie hissed to him. Then, in a more conciliatory tone: "Please."

The policeman went to his car and spoke on the radio receiver. He was watching her, and from time to time his gaze moved to a colleague of his. He finished his call and walked towards her.

"Now while we wait for Schmidtz, why don't you start by telling me what happened here?"

Handcuffs clicked onto her wrists. Another policeman held her shoulders. Charles was handcuffed too, but to the stretcher.

"What are you doing?"

"You're acting suspiciously, madam, and you are not collaborating. It's just a precaution until we understand what happened here."

"But we are not the baddies here!"

"Baddies? Are we playing some sort of game here?"

"Riemann is still there, probably still alive and..."

"Whooa, whooa, hang on. Now you are talking. Who is this Riemann?"

He waived his hand and a couple of his colleagues ran to tell the diggers about the other survivor.

"Tell him, Marie. Tell him even if he won't believe you," Charles said, lying on the stretcher and waving away a nurse.

Marie was fighting an internal struggle. She was so tired, she didn't want to tell the story, especially to this policeman who obviously wouldn't believe her.

"Yes, Marie, tell us the truth," said the policeman with an even more suspicious tone.

102

An abandoned warehouse collapsed in the middle of the night. Two survivors in clear shock, no clear answers, mention of a truth that others won't believe, a "baddy" still alive under the rubble. Something smelled fishy there and he wasn't smelling the old fishery when he thought that.

No sound came from the rubble, but everyone stopped what they were doing and started listening nevertheless. The men with the shovels stopped their motion in midair. The dog stopped barking and policemen, nurses, firefighters and simple bystanders looked at the rubble and waited. Something was happening, brewing underground. They could hear a humming, a vibration that could be felt only through the bones. Ears were useless in these cases, your body was an antenna.

Marie ducked instinctively and Charles turned his body so suddenly that the stretcher flipped sideways and he found himself facing the ground. Just in time for the big bang that followed. A shockwave expanded from the centre of the rubble and hit everyone and everything for a hundred-metre radius. Anyone who was not behind a wall, a car or an ambulance was dead. The ambulance protected Marie, Charles, a nurse and the questioning policeman. Other survivors scattered away after a few seconds in all directions, only to be hit again by a second wave. The policeman was still, his mouth in awe, his simple mind not fully grasping what had just happened. He felt Marie's hands on his belt, rummaging inside the small pouch where he kept the keys. He let Marie do what he knew she was trying to do. Subconsciously he understood something, and knew that Marie wasn't the "baddy" at all but a victim, like all the people who had died in the waves.

She managed to find the keys in the pouch but they fell. She dropped to her knees and took the keys, and had started to play with the handcuffs' lock when another shockwave exploded. This time even bigger than the previous ones. She felt something wet, warm and heavy on her shoulder. She decided to focus on the handcuffs first and then on what had landed on her shoulder. She opened them, and she immediately reached for the shoulder. She found something warm and wet to her touch but she couldn't know she was holding part of the facial skin of the policeman until her eyes went up and saw his headless body still standing next to her. The wave had also cut the roof off the ambulance and a garden wall behind them, and who knows how many metres farther it had travelled.

She reached for the keys again and helped Charles, who was still lying on the wet ground, face down and stretcher upside-down. She tried to do it as quickly as possible, as she knew the next wave might be fatal for everyone. She helped him stand and pulled him as far away from the rubble as possible. They ducked behind a brick wall. A nurse was still close to the ambulance in a state of shock, her eyes like perfect spheres coming out of their sockets. Marie waved with a hurrying hand so she could follow them behind the wall, but there was no response. Her mind wasn't receptive to any stimulus anymore.

Then from the rubble a pillar of light cut through to the sky. A human figure enshrined within it levitated upwards, arms stretched and chin up. His non-Euclidean forehead scar like ancient lettering inscribed in stone was burning in flames. An immanent evil god, ripe for annihilation, was born from the dust.

"He looks very pissed off," was Charles's comment.

There was no way to save the nurse. She became part of the ambulance and the ambulance became part of her in a non-Euclidean deadly intercourse.

"Run, Marie, run!" Charles shouted, pulling her hand.

She followed him, although she felt like it was all useless. They were playing the part of the prey in the never-ending chase between predator and prey. Riemann saw them and floated rapidly towards them, his head forward like a rocket bound for the upper spheres of the cosmos.

Death was upon them.

# Chapter 9
## Deus ex Machina

Then, when you thought that your entire world was going to crumble, that your life was going to be terminated, that you were not going to see your loved ones anymore; in those moments there he/she comes, the hero to save the day. Like in the comics, a *deus ex machina* that changes everything and rewrites the story.

Their hero that day was Nikola Tesla.

It all started with a phone call weeks before. Tesla was invited by the university to give a lecture on electromagnetism, when a janitor slid into the lecture hall and stood next to the door. He immediately understood that something was wrong and stopped the lecture. The janitor stepped up onto the footboard where he was standing. He whispered in his ear. Then Tesla looked at his pocket watch and grinned.

"And that is over for today, gentlemen. I hope you enjoyed my lecture, and if you have any questions please do not hesitate to write to this address."

He took the chalk and wrote his laboratory address on the blackboard. At first no one stood up, not knowing what to do. There were still twenty or so minutes to the end of the lecture and his explanation for the alternating current was halfway through and unfinished. Then, when he started to pack his bag, it became clear to all of them that the lecture was indeed over.

Tesla waited for all the students to leave the hall. Then he followed the janitor to the main office. Once inside, the old man pointed to the secretary who was holding the phone receiver.

"Urgent," she said, without any details.

On the other end of the phone was the voice of his assistant, who was working full-time in his laboratory. He said something that could not be believed.

"I'll be there as soon as possible," he said hastily.

The secretary looked at him and took the phone receiver in her hands.

"Is everything alright, Professor Tesla?" she asked, knowing her question was rhetorical. Something had obviously happened, something that had shocked Tesla making his face white.

"Ehm, I just need to go to the lab. I'll see you for the next lecture in a week's time. And for the thousandth time, I'm not a professor."

He drove as quickly as he could and found his assistant waiting for him outside the laboratory. He was a very tall and emaciated young man. He was wearing a tweed jacket over a white shirt and wiry spectacles were clinging to his pointy nose.

"No sign of burglary," he said, showing the immaculate door.

The boy opened the door and they moved into the laboratory, and found everything intact and right in its place – apart from the giant coil. There was a massive space in the lab where the coil was supposed to be. It had been in that position for the past three months. He literally ran into the middle of the empty space and spun on his feet a couple of times, like he was the main dancer of a ballet. He touched the bricks on the wall.

"None have been touched, sir," the boy said, anticipating his thoughts.

The roof?

The boy's gaze followed his chin up.

"That neither."

The floor?

106

"Only a short trace where the wheels were, but it's hard to say whether it was done last night or by us when we were building it."

Nikola Tesla sighed and sank down to the floor with a thumb. He sat for several minutes, his eyes fixed nowhere in particular, his lips slightly opened and quickly drying up. His face was still white and his index fingers were quivering a bit. His giant coil had disappeared into thin air during the night, and he couldn't understand how.

"Sir?" asked the boy.

"Yes."

"Shall I call the police?"

***

The morning after, the police chief called him again and asked another series of stupid questions. Nikola hung up almost immediately. He was tired of the questioning. The day before they had kept him for five hours.

"So professor, can you describe to me again what this *foil* is all about?"

"Coil. It's called a coil. It is an electrical transformer resonant circuit."

"Ah well, that thing. Yeah, but what does it do?"

"It is used to produce high voltage AC current. That prototype in particular was supposedly able to produce hundreds of thousands of volts."

"How does it look like?"

"It's a ten-metre-high metal column with a smooth metal toroid at the top."

"A toroid?"

"A doughnut," said Tesla, almost hissing.

The agent wrote *doughnut* on his papers.

"And are you sure it was stored in that room?"

"For God's sake, agent: it's a ten-metre and three-ton piece of equipment. One does not simply move it around the department. It was supposed to stay there once built. The only way to get it out of that room was to dismantle it."

"So someone could have dismantled it during the night then?"

"Impossible."

107

"Why?"

"First of all, someone had to use the keys for..."

"I know a lot of burglars who would surprise you for their Houdini skills. They can pass through doors and you wouldn't even notice."

"Fine. The lock argument is not that conclusive. It took us five men and a couple of days to mount the coil. You need a set of cranes as well. I would have expected all the other equipment and furniture to be moved away before dismantling the coil. To make room for the mobile cranes, of course."

"Where are these cranes?"

"There aren't. The department does not own them. We would have needed to hire them. And a van or possibly a big truck to move them in and to load the components of the coil once dismantled."

The agent wrote down most of his sentences.

"Also, most importantly, you *need* to know how to build it in order to know how to dismantle it."

"And who knows this?"

"A physicist with good knowledge of electromagnetism."

"How many out there that know about electro... *pragmatism*?"

"Very few I can think of."

"Do you have any enemies, Professor Tesla?"

"Many."

The agent didn't show any surprise.

"Then we will start to go through your *enemy list* first, professor. Please, write them down on this piece of paper and give it to the secretary. We will start to question these people first."

Nikola nodded while taking the pencil and the paper.

"One last question, professor: why would anyone steal your precious coil, Professor Tesla?"

"To either destroy my reputation or use it."

"Let's focus on the use of it. What would they use it for?"

"I don't know, but I think I know how to detect it if and where it is turned on."

And that was what he had been trying to do since early that morning, despite the third or fourth phone call he received from the police station. In front of him, on a blackboard fixed to the wall in his office, all the phone numbers and addresses of the US powerplant companies. The whole US power grid. His theory was that if someone had turned his coil on, he would have seen a peak of power in the grid. He called most of the powerplants' directors on the East Coast. He knew most of them, by the way. He asked them to report any unusual peak in usage in their area, or any sudden drop of power in a district. That coil, if turned on, would have dropped the power of all the nearby houses of a district, such was its hunger for power. A dark lighthouse, a negative beacon that would have led him to its thieves.

Thieves. Who and how many? And most importantly, why? Over the following days, the police agent had told him that all the questioned academic "enemies" had an alibi for that night. So the names that he wrote on that list were probably innocent. But who else then?

He clung to that question for the next few days, waiting for a phone call from any powerplant company. It was not only about who, but also how. How did they get in, and how did they *get it out*? There were no signs of burglary, no signs of movement. Teletransportation? How could he, a man of science, believe in such nonsense?

Then, he received a call. It was from one of the powerplant companies. But it wasn't to tell him about a sudden change in the power grid.

"So, beside producing electricity, we also distribute cables and machinery to this company in Europe. And the other day they requested more machinery to build a bigger powerplant. Apparently because they'd recently had some clients using a lot of energy, unexpectedly."

*Bingo.*

But how was it possibly in Europe? It would have taken weeks to transport it across the Atlantic by boat. Unless teletransportation… he didn't even want to think about that. Also, after the German victory during the Great War, movement of goods between the two shores of the Atlantic had become problematic. With London, its main ally in

109

Europe, reduced to dirt, Washington had started an isolationist policy and increased controls and tariffs.

"If you want, I can spell the name of the city. Ready?"

He wrote down the letters, and in the meantime his eyes were navigating the world map he had on the left-hand wall. His finger moved onto Germany: Gottingen.

"Riemann," he whispered.

There was no doubt now that what had happened to his coil and what had happened months ago during what was referred to as the Gottingen Accident were linked. He had followed all the news about Riemann's revolution. That crazy man and his henchmen playing with "dark physicks", as they called it. Quite a few of his colleagues were involved in the riots in Gottingen, and at least two professors he knew died in the blast. There were rumours that Riemann used a coil, a Tesla coil, to ignite the blast that killed and maimed hundreds of people. He couldn't understand how that could have worked, but of course he was no expert in non-Euclidean geometry.

Before going to the airport, and just minutes after he had bought the flight tickets, he opened a wooden box he had stashed in the laboratory. A crate with a handle and with a lock. He brought it with him on the plane.

\*\*\*

The car screamed all the way until it reached them. Marie thought she was going to die, not killed by the godlike wrath of Riemann but by a common car on the road. *What a disappointment*, she thought, closing her eyes and accepting *that* death.

The car's tyres shrieked on the asphalt just before Maria's and Charles's eyes. Its headlights were like owl's eyes cutting through the night. They saw the driver's door opening, a shoe and a leg down, a giant gun on the man's shoulder and then blue and violet sparks engulfing the whole road. Arcs of blue energy reached up to them, to the streetlights, to the windows high in the houses, to the side alleys, to the dark sky above them. The whole road was lit up with blue sparks, and then a shout.

"Get down!"

110

She didn't think twice as she obeyed the stranger's order, pulling Charles down with her. A blue light beam shot out of the big gun and, passing parallel to the ground, hit Riemann while he was still flying towards them. An explosion of blue and purple sparks and violet arcs lit up the night like it was day.

"Get in!" The same voice gave another order.

The rear passenger door now sprung open. Marie and Charles jumped in. The man kept staring at the spot where the explosion had taken place. It was as if he wanted to make sure Riemann was finished. But he wasn't, of course. They saw Riemann alive, first on his knees then standing up facing the car's headlights. Although he was blinded by the light he started to walk towards it, faster and faster.

The man got into the driver's seat, put the gun on the passenger seat and closed the door.

"We need a plan B, then," he said, reversing and revealing his face to Marie and Charles for the first time.

He was a middle-aged man, with thin and well combed dark moustaches. He was speaking in English but with a vague Eastern European accent. His gaze never met them, as if they were just a detail of secondary importance in the whole scene. The car accelerated in reverse up to a certain speed. He wanted to find a wider spot so he could turn it, but the road was a single lane with high brick walls on both sides. Marie could see Riemann accelerating too. He was running like a sprinter in a hundred-metre competition. He would have reached them in a few seconds if the car hadn't suddenly turned and allowed them to get up enough speed to leave him behind. The car swerved on the road, hitting the kerb several times.

Marie sighed with relief. She couldn't believe they'd been saved by this stranger. She didn't even know who he was.

"And you are...?"

He didn't reply immediately. He was continuously looking at the rear-view mirror with unease.

"My name is Nikola Tesla, nice to meet you," he said, not knowing whom he was talking to.

Obviously both Marie and Charles knew who he was.

"The inventor? That Tesla?" she asked.

"Ah, so I'm famous in Europe now!" he said with a veil of sarcasm.

"I guess we have to thank you for saving us."

"No problem. I came to kill that bastard, but that doesn't mean leaving civilians to be killed. You were very lucky I found you before he did. Why was he chasing you?"

Marie looked at Charles and smiled.

"Well, it's a long story..."

A bump from behind, like another car had crashed into them.

"Maybe a story for later. That bastard doesn't give up."

Nikola Tesla threw all his weight onto the accelerator and leaned forward, his chin touching the steering wheel. Another bump, this time with some metal scratching involved. Marie saw Riemann's hands grabbing the boot of the car. Riemann was now attached to the car, even though they were driving at eighty miles an hour.

"Get down!" Another order not to be disobeyed.

Nikola's arm stretched out into the back of the car, holding the big gun. He shot twice and the beam smashed through the rear window and hit Riemann in the face. Or at least they thought it did. Not a single scar on his face, not a burn. His grin growing in evilness.

"Shit, this guy doesn't want to die. I'll have to boost the death ray gun power. But I'll have only one shot."

Marie couldn't believe her ears. She thought the death ray gun was a myth. He'd managed to build one, then.

"Do either of you know how to drive?"

"Yes," said Charles, after minutes without talking.

"Then hold the wheel, old man."

Charles jumped forward into the passenger seat. Then he took the steering wheel, while Nikola moved back with the gun. The car decelerated abruptly without a foot on the accelerator. Charles quickly sat and pushed the pedal down, so the speed returned to what it was earlier. They were driving through main roads now, aimlessly. Charles decided to veer onto a side road that he thought would lead them outside of the city. It fishtailed and the tyres wailed on the asphalt.

Nikola was now in the rear seat. He was holding the gun down and was playing with a small valve. Marie saw a gauge going up to a red limit. He was charging the gun to its maximum. Riemann was still attached to the boot of the car. Now he had his feet on it as well. The scar on his forehead was glowing red, a sign that he was preparing to shoot an anisotropic wave. Marie tried to tell Nikola just that but things got out of hand too quickly. The car hit a pothole and it went up and down like a hiccup. Riemann's wave was shot, but luckily went skyward. Nikola didn't notice what had happened. Marie took his arm and shouted at him.

"Be quick or he will kill us!" her finger pointing at the furnace of Riemann's forehead.

Nikola realised that something was happening and pointed the gun at Riemann's head, but it was too late. They never knew if it was another pothole or Riemann's wave or a combination of the two, but the end result was destructive nevertheless. Charles lost control of the car. It literally flew and twisted in mid-air. Marie and Nikola couldn't hold on to anything and they were catapulted outside of the car. A bush was their saviour. They saw the car rolling and rolling until it stopped next to a big oak. Nikola was the first to run in search of Charles. Marie followed quickly after, limping quite badly. They thought they were going to find a bloody corpse.

"Are you alright?" he asked, finding Charles still conscious and with just a bloody forehead.

"Yes, and by the way my name is Charles Darwin," he said very calmly.

Nikola Tesla didn't say anything, unsure if he was talking to the living dead. Then that name rang a bell.

"That Charles Darwin?"

"Yep."

"And I'm Marie Curie," she said behind him, giving her hand to shake.

They shook hands with him in turns. There was silence as it was a very odd moment. They had escaped death (that day many times, too many times to make it possible, Marie thought) and now they were introducing themselves like gentlemen before the starting of a very posh horse race.

Of Riemann there was no sign. They were in the middle of the countryside in the dark, the only lights the half crescent moon and the many stars above them. In the

113

distance they could see Gottingen. There was no time to waste, and Nikola went in search of the death ray gun near where he had landed. It was a group of bushes, some with thorns and dry twigs that could cut your skin quite easily. When he found it, it wasn't for long as a dark beast jumped out of the bushes and assailed him. It wasn't human, nor animal. Its non-Euclidean features didn't belong to this earth and human words weren't enough to describe it. It was a mass of geometric impossibilities and curves that could trick the eye at any moment when it was moving. You thought you saw a hyperbole, a second later it was a torus, then it was coming towards you, then upwards. A magma of inconceivable madness but one which Marie and Charles knew the origin of: deep inside the everchanging intricacies they recognised the burning formula that was in Riemann's head. Riemann's final transformation was before them and it was ugly and shocking.

Nikola was immediately slapped away by an ultrahuman limb and flew away into the trees. Then Riemann moved his mass of non-Euclidean geometries towards the car, next to which Marie and Charles were still standing. Where Riemann's limbs touched the ground it became a forest of non-Euclidean shapes. Each footstep transformed the soil and the stones into a battleground between reality and non-Euclidean geometry. It was like witnessing the birth of non-organic plants and flowers from the very bottom of his paws (*paws* did not seem appropriate to use as a noun, but *feet* wasn't either). The trail left behind then started to die out, like an accelerated rotting process, leaving only ashes.

Marie froze in place and Charles didn't even get out of the car. The monster was upon them and it was advancing slowly and strangely without a sound. The usual sounds of the countryside filled the air, cicadas and some nocturnal bird far away. But Riemann wasn't making a single noise, as if he was inside a vacuum bubble.

Then he reached the car, and when he touched it with one of his many limbs the metal curled up and the boot arched backward and took on non-Euclidean shapes that no human could name. Charles sneaked out of the car, foreseeing that he might meet the same fate as the car.

A blue light fluoresced in the night, appearing from Riemann's back like a halo. They could smell ozone in the air now. The beam of the death ray gun hit him in the back. His non-human form arched backward, limbs in the air like the tentacles of an otherworldly alien octopus. That was pain, expressed not with crying and grimacing, but still pain. Nikola was shouting in the distance, mostly swearing and mentioning revenge. But Riemann wasn't dying. He was suffering but not disintegrating. He turned and faced the gun beam directly. He was protecting his burning non-Euclidean scar with his limbs and so Marie had an idea. In her mind she immediately understood that the gun beam would not be able to harm him unless it was directed towards the scar. There was no time to explain that to Nikola Tesla. There was no time for anything, really. She instinctively sprinted forward and threw herself inside the forest of tentacles and hyperboles. Riemann didn't stop, he was fully concentrated on Nikola Tesla. She found herself enshrouded within shapes her mind could not understand. She closed her eyes and climbed where she thought the original human head was. She then placed her hands on it and released all the energy she could. Her hands became yellow and then red, she could feel the heat and the flesh burning. She didn't know whether it was hers or his. She just continued and she wasn't surprised that she felt no pain, for she knew that was her last effort in life. There was no pain, just relief. She knew it was a sacrifice but she didn't care. Her life was at an end and it was beautiful to use her last hours to save the world. Like a heroine, like the comic heroes that Erwin loved. Her last thought was Erwin's smile.

Nikola didn't realise what had happened until Charles ran towards him screaming to stop with the gun. He didn't see Marie jumping on Riemann's back. He didn't see her inside him. He didn't know that the reason Riemann's limbs opened up and let his beam gun deep within was because of Marie's X-rays.

***

Her face was calm, she was almost smiling. No blood, no scars. Her chest wasn't going up and down anymore. Her pulse was over. The palms of her hands were the only witnesses to what had happened: charred and excoriated.

Charles sobbed next to her body for half an hour. Nikola watching from a distance, inhaling the fresh air of the night, sitting at the base of a tree. It had happened so quickly, so violently. One second that monster was there coming towards him in a killing spree, a second later he was gone. Pfui! Into thin air. No trace of him anywhere. Just Marie on the ground. Dead.

By targeting the scar on his forehead she had forced him to remove his limbs as protection, and thus the beam from Nikola's gun was able to hit his head. She saved them all. She sacrificed her life for them all. Nikola thought it was such a waste, especially when he had just met her. He wished things could have gone differently. He didn't know what to do with Charles. He was sobbing like a child. They must have had a hell of an adventure together. And seeing one of your mates leaving the world like this must have been terrible.

Nikola decided to let him cry, to let him unload all the grief he had in his body before approaching him. He tried to focus on the countryside sounds, the crickets, the early birds singing a few hours before dawn, the breeze through the leaves. A talking cat next to Charles.

"What?" he almost shouted, not believing his ears.

A cat was now sitting next to Charles and looking at Marie's dead body, and it was talking.

"What happened to Marie?"

Charles replied between one sob and the other: "How did you find us?"

"I managed to get out of the rubble and found destruction all around me. I understood that you were still alive and escaping when I heard a car accelerating at the end of the road. Riemann was following you. Then I lost you because you were too fast for me. I became dead for a few minutes, and when I became alive again I saw a huge cone of light and blue sparks coming from this point in the countryside."

Nikola was listening with his mouth wide open. *I became dead for a few minutes, and when I became alive again.* Was he really hearing that or was he dreaming it?

116

"She is gone, Tabby."

"I can see that."

"Also your owner, he is dead now."

"It's just me and you now, Charles."

Charles sobbed even more upon hearing those words.

"Riemann?"

"Gone, literally gone. We killed him, *she* killed him actually, and then he disappeared."

"His body probably moved to a different plane of existence, a non-Euclidean one."

"Possibly. But can't you mourn their deaths?"

"Charles, I don't think I have the capacity to do what you are doing: producing those drops of water for someone that passed away. I wasn't meant to..."

"Cry. It's called crying," said Nikola from behind them.

"And you are?" Tabby asked.

"I'm amazed."

"Nice to meet you, Amazed."

"Was it my coil being teletransported across the ocean, was it Riemann transforming into a monster, or is it this talking cat that amazes me the most from these few days?"

"I would be very honoured to hear it was the latter."

"Nikola, this is Tabby, Schrodinger's cat. Tabby, this is Nikola Tesla. His ray gun was ultimately the thing that killed Riemann."

"Nice to meet you, Nikola Tesla," Tabby said.

"Ho...how is that possible?"

"Nikola, I will explain this and other things in due time. Now, it's probably time to move Marie's body to a more dignified place."

## Chapter 10
## Farewell

The headstone read: "In loving memory of Marie Curie, scientist, wife and heroine."

Next to hers was Pierre Curie's headstone.

Charles wasn't in the first row. He was leaning on a nearby tree, observing the rite from the distance. He could recognise Konrad Lorenz, Albert Einstein (and his twin) and Maxwell in the back of the crowd with his little demon on his shoulder. He swore he saw the demon dressed in a bowtie and suit too. But it was difficult to say because of the distance, and because of the nature of the creature, restless and jittery. Apart from them there were hundreds of other colleagues of Marie's whom he could not recognise.

Nikola Tesla was there as well. He hadn't flown back to the States immediately. He wanted to pay his homage to Marie. He briefly waved his hand to Charles and Charles waved back. They'd had the opportunity to talk that morning about the coil that Riemann stole from his lab. Charles told him extensively about what happened. He didn't leave out any details, and Nikola seemed to believe him. Something that Police Chief Schmidtz did not entirely.

Schmidtz refused to write Charles's version down in the police report. He left the case deliberately open and unsolved, but the truth was that he believed every single detail Charles told him but he refused to write them down. We still don't know why, but we can only guess that he refused based on lack of logic. How can you describe an event that human words cannot describe and that human senses cannot even see and feel? Only madness can follow

118

after reading and believing those events. The report still reads "Events linked to the Gottingen Accident", or more succinctly known among the experts of paranormal circles as simply The Gottingen Accident. Below, a red stamp reads UNSOLVED. We know even less about Schmidtz himself. He left the police department after months of self-imposed silence and disappeared. His family is still searching for any sign of him.

"This is my first funeral, you know," Tabby said from the top of the tree.

"And what are your thoughts about it?"

"I'm clearly biased as I'm both dead and alive – I wonder if I should organise a funeral for my dead-half? – but I find it quite intriguing."

"How so?"

"For one thing, I don't get why you enclose the corpse in the wooden box knowing it will decompose eventually anyway. And then I don't quite understand the behaviour of the living at the funeral. Those things, the tears, I know that you shed them to communicate sadness, pain and even happiness (which is weird if you ask me!), but what's their purpose if the person you want to communicate this to is dead?"

"Welcome to the world of the irrational human mind, Tabby."

And after a pause and a smile: "I can't explain nor justify these behaviours. They belong to a part of our mind bound to our ancestral past."

"Mmm," said an unconvinced Tabby.

"Tears are probably more for the rest of the community, I guess. To convey an emotional state to others."

"So, if you were to bury a friend or relative alone, let's say on a deserted island, you wouldn't cry?"

"No, you would definitely cry, but what I'm saying is that the behaviour of crying probably evolved in a community context so you would cry anyway, even if you were alone."

"I'm still not convinced. What about the coffin?"

"That's just a delusion. You want to delude yourself that the body won't disintegrate so you hide it in there."

119

"Again, another irrational behaviour."

"Perhaps, but you are talking as if cats are masters of logic."

"I surely am."

"Fine, but the average cat isn't."

Tabby looked at the crowd at the funeral as if he hadn't heard that last comment.

"Will you miss Marie?"

Charles barely hid a tear in the corner of his eye.

"I will miss her, Tabby, yes."

"She saved the world as we know it."

"And Erwin did his part too."

"I guess I can feel the loss of my owner more than anyone else. But then again, he was the very source of my sustainment. Feeding me and changing my tray daily. I will miss all of that."

"You are a horrible being by human standards."

"Just because I don't shed tears and I miss the perks of the company of another being but not the actual being?"

"Yes."

"I can only blame you as you are my creator... pardon me, the creator of my consciousness."

"Your lack of empathy is due to inner and archaic areas of your brain that I don't know of. Otherwise, I would have humanised them too."

"Luckily you didn't, otherwise I would be doing all these irrational things you humans do, like mourning. I don't belong to the human world and I don't belong to the feline world anymore either."

"You belong to a circus."

"Mmm, maybe. Or perhaps I could teach quantum physics at the university. I'll thi

# Appendix
## Who is who

Most of the action in the story is within a fictional university in an unspecified city in a German-speaking country. Yes, the major accident happened in Gottingen and that together with the mentioning of Warsaw and France in Marie's flashbacks are the only real places that we can pin on a real map. But the places are, like the events, fictional and shouldn't be seen as the equivalent in our real world. A different timeline has developed just before WWI and our world and the novel's world do not share same characters, events and history.

As to the accuracy of the science and geometry, well, it's a New Weird story after all. What's New Weird, you might ask? Its Wikipedia page says "According to Jeff and Ann VanderMeer, in their introduction to the anthology *The New Weird*, the genre is "a type of urban, secondary-world fiction that subverts the romanticized ideas about place found in traditional fantasy, largely by choosing realistic, complex real-world models as the jumping-off point for creation of settings that may combine elements of both science fiction and fantasy."

And this is evident in the biographies of the main characters. They take some hints from their real lives (a thin paint of truth) but they mostly go their own ways, at times departing hugely from their real biographies. An example of this is Marie's education and Pierre's death. At some points I thought I would correct that to highlight the unjust treatment she had with her education just because she was a woman. But in the end, I kept it as it worked, I believe,

121

pretty well. In a way I'm sorry to have portraited one of the greatest mathematicians of all time, Bernhard Riemann, as one of the most hateful villains in the story. To all the mathematicians that read this novel, apologies. I doubt you have never heard of Moebius or Piranesi but if it is so a quick search in Google image section will help you in identifying these incredibly influential artists and their incredible creations.

***

**Marie Skłodowska Curie (1867-1934):** Polish and then French-naturalised chemist/physicist famous for her discoveries in the field of radioactivity and for being the first person to win the Nobel Prize twice. She could not attend the man-only University of Warsaw, so she had to attend the "flying or floating university", a series of informal and illegal classes held in private houses in Warsaw. Things changed when she moved to Paris and was able to enrol at the Sorbonne. In France she will meet Pierre with whom she shared the passion for science. They got married and Pierre subsequently helped her with her new research on the discovery of new elements. Pierre died in a tragic street accident in 1906 where he slipped on a road and was hit by a heavy horse-drawn cart. Marie died in 1934 from aplastic anaemia, probably contracted through long exposure to radiation.

**Charles Robert Darwin (1809-1882):** English naturalist/biologist famous for his contribution to the theory of evolution. In 1831 he boarded the HMS Beagle 5 years expedition around the world. It was during this long voyage that he started to come up with most of the principles of this theory of the evolution, through the study of different species, geology and fossils. In 1859 he published *On the origin of species* that was immediately met with both enthusiasm and controversy by the Victorian era. He died in 1882 of complications following a heart-failure.

**Erwin Schrödinger (1887-1967):** Nobel prize-winning Austrian physicist mostly famous for his work on quantum physics and his named after equation. In popular culture he is mostly famous due to the Schrödinger's cat thought experiment. Or to be more precise a paradox where Schrödinger tried to explain that the misinterpretation of the quantum theory can lead to absurd results. Like a cat that can exist in both states (alive and dead) at the same time. The thought experiment was about a cat placed in a box with a small amount of radioactive substance. A Geiger counter is inside the box as well and when triggered by the radioactivity it releases a poison that can eventually kill the cat. A radioactive substance's decay is a random process and the atoms are in a superposition state, *going to decay* and *not decayed yet*. Without opening the lid of the box there is no way to determine whether the cat is dead or alive so until an observer opens it the cat is both dead and alive at the same time. In 1938 left Austria to Ireland due to his opposition to Nazism, where he became Irish citizen. In In 1961 Schrödinger died of tuberculosis in Vienna where he retired during his last years.

**Bernhard Riemann (1826-1866):** German mathematician mostly famous for his contribution to complex analysis, differential geometry and Riemannian geometry, a type of non-Euclidean geometry. He studied at the University of Göttingen under Carl Friedrich Gauss that taught him about non-Euclidean geometry. The main point that makes the non-Euclidean geometry different from the Euclidean geometry is the replacement of the Euclid's parallel postulate, which gives rise to hyperbolic and elliptic geometries. He is considered to be one of the greatest mathematicians of all time. He died in Italy in 1866.

**Nikola Tesla (1856-1943):** Serbian and then US-naturalised inventor mostly famous among many things for the alternating current (AC) motor, Tesla coil, wireless lightning etc. Tesla was also a futurist and a believer in technology that could shape and help society. Later in life he claimed without any proof to have invented a weapon, the death ray, that would be so powerful that would end all the wars. Tesla died almost penniless in 1943 of consequences of a road-accident injuries in a hotel room of the Hotel New Yorker in New York City.

**Carl Friedrich Gauss (1777-1885):** German mathematician and physicist famous for his many contributions to mathematics and science in general, including number theory, geometry, theory of function, astronomy and magnetism. He was one of the first to theorise a non-Euclidean geometry, that his pupil Bernhard Riemann (see above) will develop later during his life. He died of a heart attack in 1855 in Göttingen.

**Maurits Cornelis Escher (1898-1972):** Dutch artist mostly known for his representation of impossible objects, mathematically inspired tessellations and hyperbolic geometry. Most of his work has connections with mathematics, geometry and the concept of infinity. After living for many years in Italy, then Switzerland he returned to the Netherlands where he died at age 73.

# Acknowledgments

This short novel could have not been written without the help and support from Dan Coxon, my editor. The author is also immensely indebted to Marco Fulvio Barozzi, Christa Bakker-de Zoete and George Ward for their feedback and advices.

Huge thanks to the many transcontinental flights that I had to endure because of work where there was no internet connection to distract me from the writing.

No gods nor kings only men

Printed in Great Britain
by Amazon

20371506R00078